PRAISE FOR ALI HAZELWOOD

"A literary breakthrough. . . . *The Love Hypothesis* is a self-assured debut, and we hypothesize it's just the first bit of greatness we'll see from an author who somehow has the audacity to be both an academic powerhouse and [a] divinely talented novelist." —*Entertainment Weekly*

"Another Hazelwood home run." —*People* on *Bride*

"*Bride* is a delight! Passionate and witty and primal in its intensity, Ali Hazelwood's paranormal debut introduces a world as intriguing as its characters. I absolutely adored this read."
—*New York Times* bestselling author Nalini Singh

"Contemporary romance's unicorn: the elusive marriage of deeply brainy and delightfully escapist. . . . *The Love Hypothesis* has wild commercial appeal, but the quieter secret is that there is a specific audience, made up of all the Olives in the world, who have deeply, ardently waited for this exact book."
—*New York Times* bestselling author Christina Lauren

"It's official. There's nothing Ali Hazelwood can't do brilliantly when it comes to writing. LOVED it."
—#1 *New York Times* bestselling author Jodi Picoult

"Ali Hazelwood is a romance powerhouse and she's put me firmly back in my werewolf era."

—#1 *New York Times* bestselling author Hannah Grace on *Bride*

"Everything I want and more in a paranormal romance novel."

—*New York Times* bestselling author Lauren Asher on *Bride*

"Whenever I want a sexy, witty, delicious romance, told in a fresh and intelligent voice, I read Ali Hazelwood. Prepare to get addicted. Each book is pure joy."

—*New York Times* bestselling author Simone St. James

"Funny, sexy, and smart. Ali Hazelwood did a terrific job with *The Love Hypothesis*."

—*New York Times* bestselling author Mariana Zapata

"Gloriously nerdy and sexy, with on-point commentary about women in STEM."

—*New York Times* bestselling author Helen Hoang on *Love on the Brain*

"STEMinists, assemble. Your world is about to be rocked."

—*New York Times* bestselling author Elena Armas on *Love on the Brain*

"This tackles one of my favorite tropes—Grumpy meets Sunshine—in a fun and utterly endearing way. . . . I loved the nods toward fandom and romance novels, and I couldn't put it down. Highly recommend!"

—*New York Times* bestselling author Jessica Clare on *The Love Hypothesis*

"Ali Hazelwood finally gives us paranormal, with her trademark humor, twisty plot, and spice that doesn't quit—buckle up."

—*New York Times* bestselling author Hannah Whitten on *Bride*

"Hazelwood unleashes her sparkling voice and wit on a paranormal Romeo and Juliet."

—International bestselling author Ruby Dixon on *Bride*

ALSO BY ALI HAZELWOOD

The Love Hypothesis

Love on the Brain

Love, Theoretically

Bride

Not in Love

Deep End

Problematic Summer Romance

Mate

ANTHOLOGIES

Loathe to Love You

NOVELLAS

Under One Roof

Stuck with You

Below Zero

Cruel Winter with You

YOUNG ADULT NOVELS

Check & Mate

Two Can PLAY

ALI HAZELWOOD

Berkley Romance
NEW YORK

BERKLEY ROMANCE
Published by Berkley
An imprint of Penguin Random House LLC
1745 Broadway, New York, NY 10019
penguinrandomhouse.com

Book design by Daniel Brount

ISBN: 9798217192335

An application to register this book for cataloging has been submitted to the Library of Congress.

Originally released as an audiobook by Spotify Audiobooks, 2024.

First Edition: February 2026

Printed in the United States of America
1st Printing

The authorized representative in the EU for product safety and compliance is Penguin Random House Ireland, Morrison Chambers, 32 Nassau Street, Dublin D02 YH68, Ireland, https://eu-contact.penguin.ie.

Two Can PLAY

Chapter 1

♡♡♡♡♡

"LET'S START WITH THE GOOD NEWS," MIKE SAYS, AND I IMMEdiately clutch the edge of the conference table to brace myself.

It's the specific combination of words—*start* and *good*—that switches on my fight-or-flight reflex. It implies that there will be an *end*, one we can surmise will be *bad*, and that's not what I want to hear from the CEO of the indie video game studio I work for. My mind, often prone to suspicion and overthinking, cannot help catastrophizing.

Slumps in sales. Impending bankruptcy. Mass layoffs.

On the streets, dumpsters burst into flames.

"You're still welcome to return home. Stay with me for a few weeks while you get back on your feet and look for a real

job." Mom's worried voice sounds crystal clear in my head, probably because Thanksgiving was just last week, and she had the opportunity to rehash her talking points multiple times over a five-hour dinner. *"Viola, you can't really believe that designing video games will pay the bills in the long term."*

And yet, when I glance around the conference room, the rest of the core team broadcasts excitement, *lots* of it, and no panic. It dials down both my fight *and* my flight. Clearly, I'm being overcautious. FlyButter Studios is doing great. Better than ever, in fact. Six months ago we released our most successful game to date, selling millions of copies. I was among its lead designers. My job is safer than it's ever been.

Not to mention, a major US video game publisher just invited us to submit a proposal for—

"StarPlay got back to us regarding our ideas for the *Limerence 3* game," Mike says. His eyes circle the table and come to rest on me. It makes sense, since I'm in charge of that project. However, I'm not a fan of his three-second dramatic pause, which I spend perched on the edge of my seat, contemplating whether to strangle him. Until he continues, "And they believe we are the right people to develop the new game."

Suddenly, the conference room sounds like Coachella. FlyButter's core team is small, fewer than ten people, but we can make some impressive noise when there's something to celebrate. People clap and whistle. One of our programmers even stands for some quick flossing. It's a rare moment of joy in an industry that's mostly energy drinks sipped late at night while wailing over ergonomic keyboards.

"I don't have to remind you that the *Limerence* franchise is an incredibly hot property," Mike goes on once the cheering has died down, "and that StarPlay has been in talks with several other studios. So it really speaks to your talent that we were able to impress them with our work."

My gaze catches Ethan's. Like me, he's a game designer, and he and I have been close friends since our first year of college, when we nearly flunked out of a software engineering class because we were too busy . . . talking about video games, for the most part.

He knows, better than anyone else in the room, that The Limerence Saga books were my favorite while growing up. Some of my most cherished memories involve my dad reading them aloud and pointing at the black-and-white illustrations of the first editions—and nearly two decades later, after his eyesight took a turn for the worse, me doing the same for him. When Ethan and I heard that StarPlay, the publisher holding the licensing rights, was thinking of developing the third installment in the game series based on the saga, we immediately started lobbying to have our name in the ring.

I may have taken the lead position when it came to developing a proposal for this project, but Ethan was with me every step of the way. There were a lot of early mornings and late nights to make the deadline—so many that our colleagues at FlyButter started wondering whether we were carrying on a secret affair—but all that work clearly paid off.

Ethan grins at me, and his hand lifts in a high five. I clap back, elated—until Mike cuts through the clamor and continues.

"The catch is . . ."

I stiffen and reclutch the table. Here it comes. The *bad* news.

"StarPlay would like to do something different from the first two games. The audience has changed, the tech has evolved, the market has expanded, yada yada. They're thinking of adding a significant combat component, which . . . Well, I don't have to tell you guys that our strength lies more on the role-play side of gaming." Mike scratches the back of his neck, like what he's about to say is giving him psoriasis. "As I mentioned, there were other teams in the running to develop the *Limerence* franchise. One of them is Nephilim Studios, and as you all know—"

A loud snort interrupts him. It overlaps with several grunts, a muttered "Those fuckers," and a swell of murmurs expressing varying degrees of discontent. Our quality assurance manager looks like he might spit on the floor at the mention of Nephilim. I glance around the room, half expecting someone to make the sign of the cross, but Mike spreads his arms to shush the protests and powers through.

"—and *as you all know*, Nephilim recently put out *Zephyr's Blade*, which was *the* combat game of the year. Naturally, they are not as experienced as we are when it comes to role-playing, which is why StarPlay had the, um, unorthodox idea of asking whether *we* could team up with *them* and—"

"No." Shannon, our character artist, bursts out of her chair as if intending to flee the premises. The rest of my colleagues remain sitting, but heads are shaking, upper lips are curling, breaths are *gasping*, and—

"Quiet," Mike orders, and the room hushes. He's usually a relaxed, easygoing boss, but he surveys the room with such a stern expression, I'm a bit scared. "Do I have to remind you that we are a midsized studio? We're in the black now, but every time we develop a new game, we run the risk of the product not being a hit and going bankrupt. You know what kind of opportunity StarPlay's funds would afford us. The influx of cash that would come with producing a *Limerence* game could carry us for years. So if you could take a seat, *Shannon*."

Shannon does, fully pouting. The room falls into silence, and Ethan clenches a hand around his mug, like he's considering throwing it across the room. Instead he says, surprisingly calm: "The thing is, we know most of the guys at Nephilim. They're not exactly . . . There is history."

"I am aware. And so is StarPlay. And so is Otto, the head of Nephilim." Mike drops the name casually, as though we're not all aware that Otto and Mike are decade-long fuckbuddies. They're spotted sneaking in and out of each other's hotel rooms about once per convention. Well, Mike sneaks. Otto just struts around, usually holding a box of condoms.

"It's a small industry," Mike continues, "and some of you have, um, worked with Nephilim's employees in the past, been in relationships with them, or had"—he side-eyes at Shannon—"run-ins of other kinds. The compatibility between our teams is a valid concern, and we've been discussing ways of establishing whether a collaboration is possible. And that's why we've come up with an idea." A single deep, fortifying breath. "A few weeks ago, I asked you to block off a few days in the middle of December for a FlyButter team retreat."

"No," Shannon whispers, quickly shaking her head. Beside her, Ethan covers his mouth. Mila, our sound designer, looks on the verge of a syncopal episode. Everyone else blinks in stunned silence.

"Yes. We have decided that the core team of Nephilim will join us at the cabin, and—"

"But why?" Shannon asks.

"—*and* we'll see if we can get to a place where a professional collaboration is feasible. We'll have a few days to focus on team building, group development, stuff like that. Don't make me use the word 'synergy,' you know I have no clue what it really means." He looks pained again.

"What if . . ." Mila clears her throat. "What if—and this is a real possibility—once we get to the cabin, we find out that it's all a ruse they orchestrated to harvest and traffic our internal organs?"

Mike sighs. "Given our collective lifestyles I doubt our kidneys would fetch much on *any* market."

"Is the lodge even large enough to host all of us?" A level designer asks. "If someone needs to stay home, I volunteer as—"

"It is, but nice try."

"What if we get *snowed in* with them?" Mila asks. "What if they go all *Shining* on us? What if we end up in the hot tub together and one of them farts in it out of spite and—"

"Okay, that's it. No more writing Nephilim fan fiction." Mike turns off the monitor and disconnects his iPad. "Next month. Retreat. It'll be a couple of days dedicated to mending this weird enmity we've developed with Nephilim. I want you to become friends with them. Or, more realistically, I want you to fake it till you make it and try to avoid *physical incidents*, keeping in mind that any altercation would mean no chance of working on *Limerence 3*." He stands, palms flat against the conference table. "You're going to ski a bit, sit in front of the fireplace with some expensive booze StarPlay will pay for, and by the time we come home we'll all be bosom buddies and live happily ever after. Or else. Meeting adjourned. Everyone, get back to work." He claps his hands. "Chop-chop."

It's to Mike's credit how impervious he is to the dirty looks people subject him to as they file out of the room, dragging their feet and muttering things like "evil corporate overlords," and "like we don't know he and Otto get it on," and "gonna key his PS5."

I linger in my seat, chewing on my bottom lip and trying to give a positive spin to the last ten minutes.

All that matters is that I'm not getting fired. Everything else will be fine.

Certainly.

Probably.

Maybe.

There is a slight chance that it will all be fine.

Sure, working on my favorite franchise was supposed to be a career highlight, and now it feels more like someone peed in my breakfast cereal and handed me the bowl, but—

"Thank you, Viola."

I hear Mike say my name and abruptly look up.

"I'm so glad at least *someone* is not overreacting." He smiles at me. "I know how much *Limerence* matters to you. You're the only one I trust to behave civilly."

I swallow. Try to gather enough words for a reply, but nothing comes.

"You look a bit pale." Mike frowns. "Is everything okay?"

"Of course." I paste a midsized grin on my face, grab my laptop, and spring to my feet. On my way out the door I even manage: "Everything's just peachy."

Chapter 2

EVERYTHING'S SHIT. EVERYTHING'S THE WORST. AND NOTHing, absolutely *nothing* is peachy.

Because here's the deal: If I had to transcribe the list of interpersonal issues between Nephilim and FlyButter employees, I'd use up one of those forever toilet paper rolls—and fill an interaction graph worthy of a Dostoyevsky novel.

Otto once called our tools programmer a "nincompoop" in front of an audience of thousands.

Mila used to be engaged to one of their 3D artists.

Ethan quit three months into his tenure at Nephilim because of differences of opinion on what constitutes "humane working conditions"; Shannon got drunk at GameCon and provoked a physical fight with an AI programmer who called her a "spaghetti coder"; Kai—one of our programmers—saw his mail start to mysteriously disappear when a Nephilim producer moved into his apartment complex, and this overview is not even remotely comprehensive of the varicolored ways in which our studios are pretty-feuding.

For instance, it pointedly disregards what happened between me and Jesse fucking Andrews.

Then again . . . did *anything* happen? As the days count down to the skiing retreat, I try to talk myself into believing that the reason behind the tension between Jesse and me is just some good old competition. After all, he and I are both video game designers, both damn good ones. About the same age, trying to bring new, creative stuff to the industry. We've won awards, gotten to lead teams, made names for ourselves. It would be weird if there *weren't* a touch of rivalry.

Except, that's not it. As much as I'd love to pretend that the awkwardness between us is born of joy-thieving comparison, Jesse's specialty is action and adventure, while I shine at creating characters and storylines. We occupy different places in the industry, and if *I'm* aware of that, so is Mr. Point and Click.

We originally met six or seven years ago, when I was up for my first industry position. As far as I can recall, *that* interaction wasn't bad. All I remember is being fresh out of college and walking into the last phase of an interview for a small software company here in Seattle. Jesse was already working there as a developer, and he stood to shake my hand the second I entered the conference room.

Initially, I barely paid attention to him, registering nothing more than a fuzzy impression of dark hair and thick-framed glasses. I had a migraine from staying up all night to prep, and Jesse's role seemed to be assisting the company CEO, who asked all the questions. I was there to prove to my mom that it was indeed possible to make a living, as she liked to put it, "*playing* Mario Kart," so I did my best to charm Jesse's boss, which did not work.

And ultimately, I didn't care. Not after the asshole said something about my portfolio being too "girly" to get me anywhere, gave a good chuckle, and then asked if I really enjoyed video games, or if I was just trying to impress my boyfriend.

Jesse, to his credit, stuck up for me. "*This is unprofessional. And unnecessary*," he told his boss firmly, speaking for the first time since the interview had started. But I was already standing to leave, and a gift of the golden wool shed by thirty magic llamas would not have persuaded me to stay and work for this shitty, shitty man.

So I walked out. And Jesse followed—I do recall that. He jogged after me, quick and long-legged, and once he caught up, he stood over me with concerned eyes. He made sure that I was okay and apologized on behalf of . . . men, presumably? I accepted—and *may* have vented at him for the next twenty minutes. But Jesse took it in stride, giving me some great advice about my portfolio and pointing me in the direction of this new game studio that was hiring at the time—FlyButter. *A decent human being in this blighted industry*, I told myself. I thanked him, said goodbye, and didn't think of him again until a year or so later, when we crossed paths at a local game expo.

By that point, the company I'd interviewed for had gone bankrupt—proof that a just god might, in fact, be milling about. I was now with FlyButter, while Jesse had gone on to become lead designer at Nephilim, with a growing reputation as a third-person action-adventure superstar. On the second day of the con, I spotted him at a panel on backward compatibility. Watched him rise from his chair to offer the seat to an older man in the audience.

Immediately recognized him.

The glasses were still there, with the same dark, square frames. His black hair, though, was styled in a shorter, low-maintenance cut. He was tall, even taller than I remembered, wearing jeans and a dark hoodie—the uniform of every other guy in attendance. He stood in the back of the room with his arms crossed, and as I studied him, I realized something that I hadn't been in the position to pay attention to during our first meeting.

Jesse Andrews was cute.

Very cute.

Handsome, really.

I resent the stereotype that most of us gamers are basement-dwelling trolls with pee buckets under their desks—eldritch horrors with no choice but to find refuge in computers. We tend to be perfectly normal-looking. Jesse, though, might have been a bit more exceptional than that.

In my couple of years in the gaming industry I'd seen enough relationships dissolve into emotionally dysregulated drama to know that any kind of workplace entanglement should be strenuously avoided. And yet . . .

"Why are you smiling dopily in the direction of Jesse Andrews?" Mila asked, elbowing closer to me. "Is he like, your drug dealer?"

"I'm not . . ." I frowned. "Was I really doing that?"

"Yup."

"Damn," I muttered. I glanced at the stage, where someone was doing a mic check ahead of the panel.

Mila leaned in. "Should I introduce you?"

"Oh, no . . . I already met him. Once."

"Cool. I went to high school with him. Same homeroom during senior year."

"Really?" I couldn't help asking, "How was he?"

"Really nice, actually. He was the captain of the soccer team, so you'd expect some douchiness, but he was a great guy. The first time I got drunk he held my hair while I puked and then sat down with me to play *Grand Theft Auto* while I sobered up. And he always let me copy his trig homework."

"Yeah." I nodded, unsurprised. "When I met him, he was really lovely to . . . Mila, what are you—"

"I haven't talked with him in a while, let's go say hi!" She pulled me by the forearm, tugging me toward Jesse. "I need to ask him how he came up with the emu Easter egg in *Forbidden Forest*!"

"I'm not sure . . ." But we were already there, by Jesse's side, and he was bending down to hug Mila and greet her warmly, making her laugh as he explained—with a healthy dose of self-deprecation—that he hadn't gone to their five-year reunion because he wasn't ready to find out whether he'd peaked in high school. Then she pulled back, and his gaze fell on me, the silent friend loitering nearby, and . . .

For a second, he went so incredibly still, I thought, *Thank god he remembers me.* It was, paradoxically, in the way his eyes *didn't* widen, his lips *didn't* curl, his posture *didn't* shift. It was all too absent to indicate anything but recognition. And yet, when Mila said, "And you know Viola, right?" his too-handsome, square-jawed face arranged into something blank.

A tense pause followed. Eventually, Jesse opened his mouth to say who knows what, but Mila must have picked up on his hesitation, because she added, "At least, that's what Viola told me." Mila lifted an accusatory eyebrow at me, as though lying about being acquainted with rising industry celebrities was a notorious pastime of mine, and I wished for the underworld to swallow me and for its dwellers to stab me.

"Yeah. We met at that interview for . . . You know what, never mind." I waved a hand, like it didn't matter that I was the opposite of memorable. My heart was racing. *Why* was my heart racing? "I'm Viola Bowen. From FlyButter. Which you recommended I apply to when—"

I got interrupted when a serious redhead (Otto, I'd later find out) came to fetch Jesse for something or other of international tactical importance. Jesse left quickly, with a last smile for Mila, a promise to get coffee with her soon, and not a single ounce of attention paid to me. I stared at his straight back as he walked away, wondering whether I was self-centered enough to be offended, and didn't tear my eyes away until Mila began making weird noises.

I turned around and found her sniffing me. "What are you doing?"

"I was just curious."

"About what?"

"Whether you smell."

"Why would I—"

"Jesse sure seemed to not like *something* about you. Maybe you stink?" She shrugged, joking, yes, but . . . maybe not fully.

Part of me was glad to have confirmation. The other . . . the other didn't want to admit to being disliked. "What? No. We just got interrupted."

"Uh-huh. The other time you guys met—was that by any chance when you ran him over?"

"What? No."

"His dog?"

"No."

"His mother?"

"No!"

"Okay. I bet I imagined it. I'm sure he does *not* want to staple your forehead."

I was sure, too. Mila had a flair for the dramatic, but the truth is, assuming that someone dislikes you based on a one-second interaction requires a degree of narcissism that I'd rather avoid. So I moved on, put the whole incident out of my mind, and managed to never think about Jesse again.

Just kidding. What *actually* happened, in the following months, was that I became hyperaware of him. All of a sudden, I saw him everywhere. Not only at conferences, but in the credits of games I played, giving an interview to my favorite YouTube channel, winning indie designer of the year awards. I realized that we had industry friends in common, that he'd graduated from my college three years ahead of me, that he was very active in the labor rights group trying to unionize us at the national level.

And the more I knew about him, the more I realized that he was a pretty great guy, and—I'm not proud of it, but denying it would be a Pinocchio-worthy lie—I developed a tiny, nanoscopic, itty-bitty crush on him.

To be clear, what embarrasses me is not my fascination with Jesse Andrews, but the fact that it persisted for *years*, even in the face of his treatment of me. Or maybe I should say, *lack* of treatment? If he had been rude, or mean, he'd have lost his charm, and it would have been *so* easy to write him off as another Gamergate dudebro convinced that women's master plan was to pollute the shades of his beloved industry. But no: Jesse's primary sentiment, when it came to me, seemed to be indifference. He never approached me of his own volition. Whenever I approached *him*, he was graceful, friendly, collegial, *and* aggressively apathetic. *He's an introvert*, I told myself. Except, he was clearly capable of *extroverting* with our shared acquaintances.

Am I the problem? I wondered. Just in case, I doubled my friendship overtures—and found that my attempts at conversation were met with remarkable politeness and profound disinterest. Whenever our paths crossed, not *once* did I notice Jesse's eyes voluntarily land on me. To be clear, he never gave me reason to believe that he wanted to, say, cut me into pieces and stuff me in an all-purpose trash bag, or even that he'd pretend not to see me if I were hitching on the side of the road in the middle of the night. In fact, I never got a hint that he actively disliked me. The truth was obvious, though: I existed, and he couldn't have cared less.

And yet, I still liked him. A good old case of "wanting what you cannot have," maybe. Or it's possible that I require the help of professionals with numerous and varied medical degrees. Either way, about three years after our first meeting, following an industry dinner in which we sat across from each other but did not exchange a word past *hello*—because he was too busy chatting with some girl from Nintendo—it finally happened.

I had a sex dream.

And it starred Jesse fucking Andrews.

I woke up bathed in sweat and had to stifle a truly obscene sound with my palm, because *clearly* my subconscious's opinion of his skills in that area was very high. And it didn't stop there. In the next couple of years, always in the wake of Jesse sightings, chance encounters, or even simple mentions of his name, the aforementioned subconscious presented me with thirteen more versions of that dream. Seven of them, to my horror and guilt, occurred while I was still seeing my ex.

So I resigned myself. I was into Jesse, and Jesse wasn't into me. Whatever. Not a problem. It *was* my first unrequited crush, and it smarted a little that I'd once seen him hand a piece of croissant to a pigeon and sustain longer eye contact with it than he ever did with me, but I could deal.

As time went on, the relationship between FlyButter and Nephilim soured because of dozens of reasons that had nothing to do with me and Jesse. Everyone in the industry knew about the constant squabbling, and as they made a point of keeping the two studios apart to avoid conflict, I came across him less and less—and, blessedly, dreamt of him less and less.

And then, last winter, about six years after our first meeting, I had to finally face the truth, and it was arrestingly ugly—much uglier than I'd ever suspected.

Up until that point, all our meetings had been through work events. I'd never interacted with him in a purely social situation, mostly because I barely interacted socially with anyone. As a lead, I worked ten-hour days, more during crunch periods, and at night I wanted nothing beyond the welcoming embrace of my couch. Prying myself from my pajamas was a *feat*—one that required the promise of something particularly exciting—or, more often, something mandatory.

And that's how I finally ran into Jesse Andrews in the wild: His college roommate—now a PE teacher—was about to get married to my cousin—a baker. Not too shocking a coincidence, considering that we'd all gone to the same school. It meant that we were both invited to the engagement party they held just before the holidays—and *that* outing, I definitely could not skip.

I noticed him the second I stepped into the private room they'd rented at the restaurant—not hard, since he was a head taller than pretty much everyone else. He didn't have the same luxury, since I was average height, with long, wavy brown hair and few features that'd make me pop in a crowd. And in hindsight, I should have taken advantage. I should have faked a pneumothorax, or fulminating dysentery, and gotten the hell out. Unfortunately, I was pulled in by my Aunt Selene and subjected to the passive-aggressive line of questioning perfected by the Bowen family through generations. Had I gained some weight? It looked great on me, but I should watch my diet from now on. Was I seeing someone? There were upsides to being forever alone. Were the bags under my eyes a fashion statement? Was I any closer to finding legitimate employment? Did I know that a woman's eggs were the first thing to age?

After Aunt Selene, it was Aunt Millie. Then Uncle Max. Then a cousin thrice removed whose name I never learned. Then Mom, who tormented me with the totally *not* made-up tale of an unnamed friend's son, who had recently lost his nonspecified gaming job, become unhoused, and been eaten by crocodiles while sleeping under a bridge. Then three of my siblings, who all gave me noogies and demonstrated that in their minds I'll always be twelve years old.

It's tough, being the last of five children. My brothers and sisters are great, and I am as certain of their love as I am of the binary code, but the youngest takes plenty of shit, plenty of times. If there's a prank to be pulled, a wedgie to be given, a diary to be read out loud, I'm the one they default to. My entire life has been a study in patience and sharing—food, toys, clothes, attention, my parents' energy—which is probably why now that I'm an adult I love solitude so much.

By the time my siblings were done toying with me, nearly two hours had passed. I decided to make my way to the bride and the groom, give them my well wishes, and get the hell out. Easier said than done, since most Bowens were either buzzed or straight-up drunk.

I wove my way through the crowded room toward the exit, wondering at my family's reproductive prowess, until a large structure bumped into me. When I turned to glare at what stood between me and freedom, I discovered something surprisingly familiar.

Jesse held a beer in his hand and blinked down at me, perhaps wondering whether his least favorite industry acquaintance had turned into a stalker. Something peeked out from behind his head, something green and leafy and . . . mistletoe.

He was under it.

So was I.

And everything unraveled. Before I had a chance to explain myself, or run away, or steal Jesse's bottle, smash it against the wall, and use its jagged remains to keep my family at bay, approximately ten people related to me by blood began chanting for us to kiss.

"Mistletoe!" my cousin, the blushing bride, yelled. "Kissing plant!" I glanced at her tiara and briefly wondered what she'd do if I broke it over my knee and forced her to eat it.

"You gotta kiss!" Uncle Evan said.

"Viola, did you know"—my brother Victor interjected—"that the mistletoe—*Viscum album*, order Santalales, family Santalaceae—is an obligate hemiparasitic plant? But yes, you two should kiss."

I glanced at my surroundings as a somewhat inebriated commotion brewed around us, wondering whether someone would bring up the sheer inappropriateness of the situation. Why did families not have HR departments? I'd file the shit out of a complaint. Or ten.

But no one said anything. There were a couple of cheers, some mutterings about *tradition*, and I took a deep, resigned breath.

Okay. Whatever. Fine. It was going to be a kiss. A small one. On the cheek, probably. And while the indignity of having my family act like a frat house *did* make me want to guzzle a bottle of fungal ointment, this could have been worse. After all, I liked Jesse. I was reasonably sure he had decent personal hygiene. Plus, *after* the kiss, we could laugh together over this shitshow. It might even tip us over from indifference into . . . something warmer. Something nice.

So I looked up to meet his gaze, meaning to offer him my best *We're in this together* smile. Except that it never materialized, because I was immediately confronted with the expression on his face, and it could be described only as *disgusted.*

And that was *before* he said: "I don't think so."

This time, he wasn't friendly, or graceful, or cordial. He was abrupt and unwavering, as though the idea of kissing *me*—a known carrier of mono *and* the chicken pox—was so revolting to him, he could not bring himself to fake politeness.

And people around us picked up on it, because after a moment of silence, that was that. A handful of disappointed, "*Oh, come on, man,*" and *buzzkill* comments, but soon enough the bride and the groom were pushed in our places, and had their tongues down each other's throats, and it was over.

Kind of.

My cheeks were aflame—from the public rejection, from how quickly it had all happened, from Jesse's eyes on me, full of something that . . . It wasn't contempt, was it? It couldn't possibly be.

Or maybe it could. Because fifteen minutes later, as I picked up my jacket before leaving, I overheard my cousin's voice down the hallway. "You could have kissed her on the cheek," he was saying.

I stopped in my tracks. He and Jesse were looking out the window, facing the other way. Jesse's broad back moved up, then down in a careless shrug.

"I mean," my cousin said, "even if you don't like her, you could have been nicer about it."

"No. I couldn't."

"Why, though?"

A pause. "I don't want anything to do with her. It's better that way."

This happened nearly twelve months ago, but the frustrated sigh that followed is still crystal clear in my head, a split-second moment that I'll never erase from the cortex of my brain.

Even now—after hours, the last one lingering in the office, as I stare at my blank screen—even now I can *hear* it. Two days before leaving for the winter retreat.

"You may not want anything to do with me," I say out loud to the empty, open-plan room, "but I want the *Limerence 3* project. Where does that leave us?"

I tip my head back, stare up at the wall, and wonder whether I could ever work alongside Jesse Andrews—and vice versa.

Chapter 3

My expectations for the retreat are lower than a public school's budget, but even *I* am surprised by how poorly it starts.

It's the week before Christmas, six thirty a.m. Despite the thick hat and chunky knit scarf I wrapped myself into, I shiver in the dimly lit Nephilim parking lot. I'm wondering why we decided to meet here instead of, for instance, the middle of a cornfield, a funeral home, or literally *anywhere* else, when Mike jogs toward me and says, "Viola? Will you do me a solid?"

No, a wise, self-preserving voice screams inside my head. *Fuck, no.* But what I cautiously say is, "Depends."

He smiles as if I said yes, and I don't like it. "A tree fell last week, and parking is temporarily limited at the lodge. We're trying to drive as few cars as possible to Mount Baker, and by my count one member of our group is going to have to ride with the Nephilim guys. I'm thinking that you—"

"No," I say, this time out loud, vehemently enough that my breath puffs white between our faces.

"Please, Viola." His expression is pleading under the hem of his beanie hat. "No one wants to do it."

"Right. Well. Neither do I."

"You're my least drama-prone team member." What he means is: You're the easiest to manipulate, because you have the most to lose. We all know how important *Limerence 3* is to you.

And he's right, dammit.

Still, I say, "I can be pretty dramatic, if that's going to get me out of driving to the lodge in . . ." I cock my head, remembering that my issues with Nephilim's employees are heavily circumscribed. "Whose car?"

"Otto's, I think?"

"And who else is in it?"

"I don't know. Jorge, I guess. Aren't they dating?" There is some indisputable bitterness in his tone. I guess we now know who initiated the last breakup in the long-running Otto–Mike soap opera. "Ashley, maybe."

"The goth girl who always looks mad?"

"Yup."

Hmm. I could deal with them. "I'll do it"—I start, and Mike exhales in relief until I continue—"in exchange for three extra days of PTO next year."

He rolls his eyes. "One."

"Two. No blackout dates."

"Deal. You're saving me here, Viola." He claps my shoulder. "Thank you."

"Yeah, sure." I head for Otto's bright red hair and tall frame. I haven't had many opportunities to interact with him in the past.

"Hi." I smile. "Is it okay if I catch a ride with you?"

He shrugs, like all my existence inspires in him is mild repugnance. I don't take it personally, since he's known in the industry for his general lack of warmth. "I don't care." His British accent is tight and clipped. "But this is not my car."

"Whose . . . ?"

He points at a spot high behind me, and . . .

But of course. Of *fucking* course, it's not *his* car.

I sigh, resigned.

"Hi, Jesse," I say, before I've fully turned around, feeling almost impressed by my terrible fucking luck. Did Mike *lie* to me on purpose?

No. He doesn't know about my weird relationship with Jesse. No one does, because every time I start to explain it, I realize how paranoid and egocentric it makes me sound.

One of the most popular game designers, whom everyone loves, doesn't want to be my bestie. Woe is fucking me.

Whatever.

"Good morning," Jesse says, low and a little rumbly, like maybe he's not an early-morning person. His eyes on me, though, are fully awake. Without asking he takes my overstuffed duffel bag from my hand to easily lift it into his trunk. His dark sweater looks *thin*, and he's not even wearing a jacket, but his body exudes warmth. Meanwhile, I'm onion-layered and my teeth still chatter.

"Thank you," I say.

It's the first time we've seen each other since the mistletoe incident. The first time I listen to his voice since I overheard him say those stunningly horrible words.

"I don't want anything to do with her."

It makes my blood pressure rise, but I quickly realize that Jesse might not even remember the engagement party. He's back to his polite but frosty self, and I go settle in in the back of his car, on the passenger side, trying to curl myself into invisibility.

I must be cursed. My brother's cat, Edith, could have sicced an Egyptian goddess on me for putting her in that lobster costume last Halloween. It's the most logical explanation for this triple whammy: Not only have I been forced to invade Jesse's personal space and, I can only assume, cause him a deathly amount of displeasure, but next to me

Otto is playing *Flappy Bird* with the sound on, and Ashley, who is sitting in the front, appears to require several yards of leg space.

"Hey," I ask her with a smile. "Could you move your seat up a bit?" I'm five six. She's what, half a foot shorter? It's a fair request, I think, but Ashley clicks her tongue and adjusts the seat, giving me about a fourth of an inch more.

I sigh. "Thanks."

When Jesse comes in, his glasses fog up. Ashley plucks them from the bridge of his nose and uses the hem of her shirt to wipe them clean. Then she slides them back with a small, intimate smile that he seems to return.

Oh my god. Are they dating? Together? In love? Having sex? Is he as good at it as my dreams seem to—

Doesn't matter, Viola. Not your business.

I lean back against the headrest, close my eyes, and try not to breathe too noisily.

We arrive at the lodge three hours later, and I take in the snow-dusted pine trees and rustic wood walls while musing that since this car ride didn't kill me, it must have therefore made me stronger. I am now better prepared to conquer difficult, life-changing events. Childbirth, broken hips, hemorrhoids? I'm coming for you all.

It's hard to choose what the most unpleasant part was. Maybe when I asked Jesse to stop at a gas station so I could pee, and Otto muttered that "*there are exercises one can do to overcome poor bladder control, Viola.*" Jesse pretending that he needed to hear the traffic report and changing the radio station right after I excitedly let it slip that the song playing was one of my favorites—that's pretty high up there, too.

There were, of course, several conversations in which the three Nephilims talked about things, places, ideas, and people that are obviously staples of their lives, and that I'm not familiar with. Through those, I discovered that Jesse has a sense of humor. Jesse loves to roast Otto. Jesse is kind, and gently reassured Ashley when she was anxious about her dog having to be put under for teeth cleaning, telling her that he's had many dogs, and they all did fine during similar procedures. Jesse is lovely—and he did not look at me *once* in two hours and fifty-seven minutes.

And then there was the slow torture of Jesse and Ashley discussing in excruciating detail the training, equipment, and philosophy that underlie triathlons. I had not pegged either of them for fitness enthusiasts, but the in-depth conversation about zone 2 training and blood lactate testing and tempo runs clearly proves otherwise. When they started talking about their preferred brand of energy gels, I considered crawling out of the car and walking to the lodge.

Which, in a positive turn of events, looks nice. Much larger than I expected, charming, snow dusted. Very . . . expensive. Tall windows. Balconies and decks surrounded by trees and narrow paths. I don't think I've ever been in a place quite like this, and I instantly fall in love with the scent of the pines and the crisp air.

I'm happy to be here. And if I had to endure the eardrum-shattering noise Otto makes when slurping from a straw to reach this destination, so be it.

"Hey." Mike comes up to me and pats me on the back, his hand heavy through my thick winter coat. "Thanks again for riding with Jesse."

"No problem. Although, you said I'd be riding with Jorge."

"That's what I thought, but . . ." He lets a small, excited grin slip. "Manny told me the rumor is that Jorge and Otto had a tiff and Jorge quit on the spot."

Mike, you lovesick fool, I say—but not out loud. Because he *is* my boss. "Look at you, rejoicing in another man's unemployment."

"No, I . . . well, maybe. A little. Listen, out of everyone here, you're the only one who never had a public falling-out with someone at the other studio. You, and maybe Jesse. When people at FlyButter and Nephilim start stabbing each other with ski poles, you're going to be the last two standing."

"We'll see about that."

"Yeah, well . . . How was the drive? Did, um, Otto mention me?"

"No," I say, deciding not to sugarcoat it. "He was way too busy checking his Grindr profile every ten minutes."

Mike's eyes widen. "I—he—it's not—" he sputters and flushes. "I mean, Otto is . . . Not that it's my business, if . . ." He clears his throat. Twice. "Did you happen to catch his username?"

I shake my head and turn to my duffel—which has disappeared from the trunk. I glance around, half expecting to find it pilfered by a Sasquatch. All I see, though, is Jesse. Walking toward the lodge and carrying a bag that looks suspiciously like mine.

Chapter 4

TOGETHER, THE CORE TEAMS OF NEPHILIM AND FLYBUTTER total eighteen people—the exact number of rooms in the lodge, according to the matronly housekeeper who greets us. The large common space in which she's gathered us makes me think of those ambience YouTube videos I sometimes put on to trick my brain into thinking that I'm on vacation.

There is a large, crackling fireplace, and the smoky smell of burning wood feels like a warm embrace. I spot couches and soft, plush pillows in the seating areas, floor-to-ceiling windows that show bird and squirrel feeders, and trees so high, they must have been around for millennia. The intricate wooden beams on the ceiling make the space look timeless and immense. I have not the slightest intention of going anywhere near the skis and snowboards hanging from the rack just past the entrance—whatever part of the brain is responsible for loving rolling down a hill, mine must be defective. Still, I know I'll have a great time sticking around the cabin, letting the scent of cedar fill my lungs and the bar's hot chocolate fill my belly.

"What a nice place for a holiday," I murmur.

"And what shitty, shitty company," Ethan whispers in my ear.

I can't quite hide my snort. When Jesse and Ashley turn in the noise's direction, I pretend to be fascinated by my boots.

"You are, of course, welcome to use the facilities, including the hot tubs and the sauna on the back deck," the housekeeper informs us. I wonder if she picked up on the tension between . . . well. Everyone and *everyone.* Nephilim and FlyButter have neatly split into two very separate, very eye-contact-avoiding groups.

"You can find your room number in the welcome envelopes we gave you earlier," she continues. I glance at mine and trace the wax sigil, charmed, before breaking it open. Inside I find a single candy cane (which I immediately unwrap and stick in my mouth), an informational pamphlet, and a wooden keychain with the number 4 written on it. "Meals are buffet style, served at seven a.m., noon, and six p.m. in the dining hall."

"Which room are you in?" Ethan asks me, sliding the strap of his backpack around his shoulder.

"Four."

"Oh," he says, in a slightly subdued tone that has me pausing. By now, I can read him like a line of C++.

"What about you?" I ask.

"Eighteen." He purses his lips. "But Shannon is in three."

I smile, picturing Ethan and Shannon tiptoeing across the cabin in their underwear. They started seeing each other a month or so ago, and their relationship is so new, no one at FlyButter knows about it except for me. That's how they want it, and I get where this is coming from: Going public at work means lots of people shoving their noses into your business and dispensing unsolicited opinions. Not to mention the awkwardness if they were to break up. Their plan is to lie low and keep everything a secret until they're more stable, and I support them. However, I suspect that they'll be found out very soon if they continue making out in the copier room.

"If at two a.m. you hear someone sneaking inside your neighbor's room," Ethan tells me, "nope, you didn't."

I wonder if he'd really be *that* loud. And then I wonder if sharing a wall with Ethan's girlfriend might lead to finding out things that I do *not* want to know about my friend.

He's like a brother to me. If he has a fondness for daddy kink and milkmaid role play, he better take that to the grave.

"Actually, how about we swap rooms? That way you'll be right next to her," I offer.

"Can we?"

I shrug. "What are they gonna do? Punish us? Lock us in a lodge with our industry enemies for several days?"

He hides his laugh into my shoulder, but the sound is not quite muffled, and everyone turns toward us. "Hey, lovebirds," Mila hisses. "Housekeeper's telling us about the amenities. Hush."

I roll my eyes, because the running joke about Ethan and me being secretly in love has run its course, and tune in to hear all about the multimedia rooms.

We disperse soon after. Ethan beams and kisses me on the cheek when I drop my keys into his palm. He insists on rewarding me with his complimentary candy cane, so I chalk it up as a win. A super win, really, because rooms seventeen and eighteen are in a loft of sorts, a separate, quieter wing of the lodge that faces the woods behind the building, and I just *know* that the view from the windows is going to be breathtaking.

I hear footsteps behind me and turn to see who's going to be my neighbor for the next five days. I have no real preference, though I do hope that it won't be Otto or Mike.

There's always a chance that they'll end up rekindling things, and I do not want to find out if either of *them* has a milkmaid kink.

But, as it happens, I don't need to worry about that. Because room seventeen is not Otto's. Nor Mike's. And it's now abundantly clear that I have, indeed, pissed off a god—nay, an entire damn pantheon of gods.

I'm redefining the whole concept of *cursed*.

"Are you looking for something?" Jesse asks, coming to stand on the landing. He sounds polite, and kind, and absolutely emotionless. Like he found a lost toddler wandering the cereal aisle at the grocery store.

A milligram of good fortune would be nice, I think, taking the candy cane out of my mouth. It's clear that he's trying to keep as far away from me as possible, but he still takes up so much of the small space, it's hard to look anywhere but at him. "Nope. Well, yeah. But I found it." He stares at me like he doesn't quite comprehend, and I point to my door. "I live here."

My words set off a whole journey of emotions on Jesse's face, and I amuse myself by attempting to tease them apart. Confusion (*could this plebeian really be encroaching on my car* and *sleeping next to me?*), then worry (*will she give me the cooties?*), finally incredulity (*I will send a strongly worded email to corporate for allowing this to happen*). His expression settles on something blank and unreadable, and he says, pleasant and neutral: "I can ask the housekeeper to give me another room."

I don't want anything to do with her.

Really, I just wish I understood the reason for this. I didn't kill his damn pet reindeer, didn't bully him in high school, didn't steal his auntie's secret apple pie recipe. Seriously, his desire to avoid me is so completely unjustified, it's almost comical.

Except that I am not laughing.

"I don't snore loudly, or anything," I offer. I'm not sure whether I'm appeasing or challenging him. *Smooth things over*, a voice inside me insists—the same one that learned to play nice with four older siblings endowed with huge personalities. *You're going to have to work together. Maybe he doesn't want anything to do with you, but you can still salvage this professional relationship. Do it for* Limerence. "I don't shower in the middle of the night," I add. "And you seemed to dislike my music in the car, so you'll find it reassuring to know that I own great noise-canceling headphones."

I smile, but Jesse doesn't smile back. Instead he says, "I'll try to keep out of your way." It sounds like he's promising *me* something, and I—I don't get it. I watch his door close gently behind him, leaving me alone on the landing.

With a deep sigh, I stick the half-eaten candy cane back

in my mouth. I pick up my bag, step inside my room, and forbid my feelings from hurting.

Jesse Andrews may not want me around, but he's stuck with me for the next few days—and if things go well, a whole lot longer than that. The earlier he comes to terms with it, the better for all of us.

Chapter 5

AFTER SETTLING IN MY ROOM, I SPEND THE AFTERNOON walking around the property with some of the FlyButter crew. Dinner is a magnificent affair—lentil minestrone and sautéed vegetables and chicken potpie, accompanied by wine that, unlike the one I usually buy at the supermarket, doesn't smell like applesauce even one bit. The rice pudding is nothing to write home about, but the chocolate cheesecake is so movingly good, it takes me several seconds to gather my words once I'm done chewing the first bite.

"Fuck *me*," I say, shoving more in my mouth. "This is ridiculous."

Mila nods and forks another piece of the slice we're sharing. "Better than sex."

"Maybe better than sex with *some* people," John mutters from somewhere on my right. He's Nephilim's 3D artist, and Mila's former fiancé. They were together for half a decade and broke up following a whirlwind of mutual cheating and kitchen appliances thrown out the window. Needless to say: No, they did not "stay friends." Neither I nor she would have chosen to sit anywhere near him, but someone (probably Mike) had the stunning idea to assign place cards and force the two teams to mix, so here we fucking are.

Mila pretends not to hear what John said, but the suddenly square line of her shoulders tells me the words cut deep. I turn around to incinerate him with eye lasers that I so wish I'd developed instead of my mild nearsightedness, and when I find him sniggering like a fourteen-year-old, I decide to "accidentally" elbow my glass of eggnog and spill its contents in John's lap.

"Sooo sorry." I press my hand to my lips as he frantically wipes his pants with a napkin. "I'm so *clumsy*, you know?"

It is, by my count, the fourth Nephilim-FlyButter incident of the day. The others were a screaming match, a LOSER note slid under a door, and a stolen suitcase that mysteriously reappeared in the thicket outside. John leaves for a change of clothes, and I go back to savoring my cake. A few moments later, my phone buzzes with a text from Mike.

That wasn't very nice of you.

I look up to find his disapproving scowl pinning me from across the table, so I beam at him and message back.

> **This retreat was such a GOOD idea. I can feel FlyButter's relationship with Nephilim improve by the second.**

Mike sighs, so I send him the emoji of a dancing woman—and then immediately feel bad for him.

He's in a difficult position. As the CEO, all he wants is for StarPlay to invest in us so he can keep us on—and we, his team, are not exactly making it easy at the moment. I glance around the table and find no amount of effort being made by anyone: Despite the assigned seats, conversations seem to have clustered by company. Even Otto, instead of pushing for more harmony, is ignoring everyone in favor of his phone.

If we continue like this, there is no way we'll be able to collaborate on *Limerence 3*.

I roll my eyes and decide to be my best self: a reasonable adult with mostly regulated emotions. I wolf down the rest of my cheesecake, then turn to my right and smile at the dark-skinned girl on the other side of John's empty seat.

"Clara, right?"

She blinks at me. "Yes," she says, suspicious. Honestly, I can't blame her.

"I'm Viola. I don't know if you remember, but we met several years ago at that animation workshop that East Coast guy hosted . . ."

"The one in Tacoma?" She grimaces. "God, that was a waste of time."

"I know. I doubt that guy can make a finger trap, let alone a video game."

She laughs, and we start chatting, lingering at the table after most others have left. The retreat doesn't involve much structured time or mandatory activities, so we're free to spend the night doing what we like, and Clara, despite her dubious allegiance, is great company.

It'll be fine, I tell myself while returning to my room. *Nephilim and FlyButter can and will learn to get along. There will be some tiptoeing and individual friction, but we'll make it work. For* Limerence.

"Hey, Viola." I turn to see Mila catching up to me. "Wanna go explore the lodge?"

We make our way through a handful of entertainment rooms, counting two more fireplaces, coming across a pool table and a stack of board games that's higher than us. We find a winter garden, and a gym that is better equipped than the one down my block—for which I buy yearly passes every January, and yet barely frequent. The library smells like old books, and I genuinely did not know this many DVDs and Blu-rays still existed in the world.

As someone who has about $10K in student loans left to pay off, the extreme luxury of this place seems a little wasteful, but I'll take it.

"Why do you suppose we're doing the retreat here, instead of, say, a Motel 6?" I ask Mila, who shrugs.

"StarPlay sent us here. They're a giant company. Made of money."

"Yeah. But why spend money on us instead of . . . I don't know, buying Fabergé eggs for shareholders?"

She tilts her head to the side. "Maybe they would rather give a gift to real human beings whose skill sets they value than increasing the already abundant wealth of the one percent?"

It sounds so ridiculous, we burst out laughing at the same time.

■ ■ ■ ■ ■

MOST OF THE FLYBUTTER CREW DECIDES TO WATCH A MOVIE, but I've socialized plenty for the day. It's still early enough in the evening that I know I won't be able to fall asleep, so I put on sweatpants and a sweater and slip out of my room. I tiptoe past Jesse's room, keeping an ear out for any noises, but no light filters from under the door.

Maybe he's asleep. Maybe he's hanging out with Ashley. Maybe he put on a Grinch hat and a green thong and is climbing an Engelmann spruce. Not my business. I head down to the library, taking with me *The Sunken Heart*, the first volume of the Limerence series.

Oftentimes, video games derived from books are adaptations of huge literary phenomena, the household-name kind that spend years on bestseller lists. The Limerence Saga, though, was never a big hit. Even as the first and second games were produced and rose in fame, the books' popularity never followed. In fact, most people don't know that the source material is a collection of five novels, each more complex and beautifully written than the last.

The story starts out simply enough: Noham, a young warlock, teams up with a human girl, Aqualuna. In the first volume, their goal is to rescue her missing older brother. They succeed, albeit not without a few setbacks and a lot of bickering, and by the end of the book they both recognize that they're formidable together. The rest of the series follows the same basic formula, except that as Noham and Aqualuna grow up on the page, the worlds they visit and the adventures on which they embark become progressively darker and more elaborate.

Like me, Aqualuna was a youngest child: at once teased and unnoticed, underestimated, even forgotten for long stretches of time, to the point that it took four volumes for her family to realize she was in the habit of taking off and visiting other dimensions. Only Noham seemed to see her for who she was, and offer his unwavering support. Aqualuna never became magic herself, nor did she gain special powers, but reading the saga meant watching her blossom into a strong, independent heroine and earn the respect of those who surrounded her.

Needless to say, it all resonated very much with me, a girl addressed as "Swampy" daily by her siblings because of an unfortunate childhood accident.

My dad had loved the series since he was a boy, and decided to introduce me to it after I told him that books were boring, and that I couldn't imagine why someone would willingly *choose* to read. It quickly became *our* thing, just him and me and none of my loud, attention-hogging siblings. Every night he'd come to my room and read a chapter or two, until page after page after page I realized that books were not *that* boring—they were, in fact, the best thing ever. We raced through the volumes in just a few months, until we got to the last one.

"Once you're older," he said, "we'll read it together."

I pouted. "Why not now?"

"Because you're still a bit young for it. And that book, Vee, is a bit harder to understand." He cupped my cheek with those calloused hands I can still feel sometimes, so warm and familiar. "Don't worry, you'll be ready soon."

But by the time I became ready, Limerence was the last

thing on my mind. By then, new books had entered my life, and video games, and school and friends and boyfriends. I forgot all about Aqualuna and Noham—until a few years ago.

When Dad got sick.

"Read to me, Vee," he'd say when I visited him after work, and picking up Limerence felt as natural as breathing. We began with volume one, and it was like traveling back to the past. My love for the characters, the way their adventures transported me to faraway places, how close I felt to Aqualuna and how invested I was in her success and well-being—I was reminded of it all. Except that this time around, I was terrified we wouldn't make it to the end before Dad left me—so scared that it kept me up at night.

I shouldn't have worried, though. I still remember how it felt, reading "The End" out loud and closing the fifth book, a little shell-shocked. Running my fingers over the embossed texture of the back cover. Saying, "Dad?"

"Yeah, Vee?"

"What do you think 'limerence' means?"

"What do you mean, what do I think?"

"I . . . it's not a real word, is it?" I'd always assumed it to be a made-up term, like *irregardless* or *bootylicious* or *ornithopter*. Nothing too unusual for the fantasy genre. But now that I'd reached the end, I was puzzled by the fact that the word *limerence* did not make a single appearance in the texts.

"Oh, Vee. You should definitely look it up." His gentle

laughter slowly turned into coughing, and I dropped the topic. But that night, I did pick up the dictionary. And afterward, I could never see the series in the same way, because—

". . . just wait it out."

I hear the words drift out of the pool room and stop in my tracks. The door is ajar, but not open enough to see who's talking. The voice, though, is familiar.

John. Mila's ex.

Eggnog boy.

"Here's the deal," he continues. "If StarPlay has to choose between FlyButter and Nephilim, if it comes down to it, who do you think they'll go for?"

"I have no idea, man." Another voice, this time a woman's. Ashley. "I know you want me to say that they'd choose Nephilim, but FlyButter has done some great work recently and—"

"No, no. Guys, follow my reasoning. Who are the studios' lead designers?"

I glance around the hallway—deserted—and squeeze closer to the wooden wall, listening in.

"Jesse," another male voice says. It's *that* guy—the programmer who once got into a fight with Shannon. "And for FlyButter it's that girl, Viola Bowen."

"She's good," Ashley says.

"She's excellent," John corrects her. "In fact, she may be the best for role-play stuff. But." I hear the clank of a few balls hitting the corners of the pool table. “She has no combat experience. You know who is the best at combat design *and* also pretty good at role-play?”

“Jesse?” Ashley asks.

“Ding ding ding! So, say that at the end of this week FlyButter and Nephilim decide that we cannot work together—which is *exactly* what’s going to happen, I mean, this retreat is already a shitshow—who do you think execs at StarPlay will give the project to? To the team that can do both well, or to the team that can only do one thing?”

“That’s a good point,” Programmer Guy says after a brief pause.

“Of course it is. So my advice is, let’s wait it out. Don’t stress over the next few days. No need to make an effort to get along with FlyButter, because if things stay as they are, *we* get to do *Limerence 3*, and *they* get nothing.”

“I don’t know. That seems . . .” Ashley sounds skeptical. “Like a bit of a gamble. How can you be so sure?”

“Hey, I’ve talked it out with a few others. They all agree with me.”

“You talked it out with Otto?” Ashley asks, a little dubious. “And with Jesse?”

“Trust me,” John reassures her. “It’s what they want, too. Hang on.” Suddenly, the door closes, muffling the voices inside.

I push away from the wall, cheeks glowing with anger.

It's all I can do not to stomp my displeasure all the way to the library.

What. The. Hell.

What the hell?

I came here in good faith. Bitching and moaning, yeah, but I came all the way here with the intention of finding common ground. And all along, Nephilim was planning some shitty Scooby-Doo sabotage.

I throw the library's door open, wondering whether grabbing a dictionary and dropping it on John's head will make me feel better, but instantly recoil. I blink once, then once more, unable to process the sight in front of me.

Jesse fucking Andrews is sitting in the reading nook I noticed earlier, the one I came in with the specific intent to use, the one I've been thinking of as "mine" for the past hour. He's relaxed in the plush chair, long legs spread comfortably, knees apart, looking way too damn cozy for my taste.

Aside from my very inappropriate dreams, this might be the first time I get a good look at him without his glasses, and . . .

I take a step back, because it's a true Clark Kent situation. Not that I subscribe to the *glasses make a person less attractive* crap '90s comedies tried to peddle, but with no obstacles between my eyes and his face I cannot help tracking the entirety of his bone structure, and I don't love it. I really don't enjoy knowing that Jesse Andrews, game developer extraordinaire, could have a respectable career in modeling.

I prefer him bespectacled.

Actually—I prefer him not existing at all.

"Are you okay?" he asks, nonplussed.

I know why he's asking. I'm overheated. Jittery. My hands tremble so hard, I have to clutch my book like it's a rescue rope. And I'm wearing the clothes I usually put on Sunday morning to go grocery shopping while the acceptable section of my wardrobe is busy frolicking in the washing machine.

Still, he can fuck right off.

"Kinda pissed, actually."

Jesse straightens, reaches for his glasses and slides them back on, as if to study me more closely. "Viola? Have you been drinking?"

"Have I been—" I sputter, and then stop. Inhale through my nostrils. He doesn't *get* to call me by name. "You know, Jesse, since last year—and even before—I've been wondering why you were so cold to me. I've expended a frankly embarrassing amount of energy figuring out what I'd done to you to deserve being ignored at best, and treated like I'm a poisonous mushroom who dared to grow on the outside of your stupid raised bed at worst."

A beat. He stares blankly at me. "I live in an apartment complex."

"And?"

"I don't have a garden."

"I don't care if you—" I grit my teeth. "Jesse, if this is how you and your buddies want to play it, I'm going to warn you right now that there's plenty of eggnog in this world, waiting to be spilled in the laps of plenty of assholes, so—"

"Viola." He stands, and in the blink of an eye he towers over me, giving me a micro-flashback of the mistletoe, when he looked down at me and for a split second, I thought that we might—

"What are you talking about?"

I take a step back. Swallow. "I heard them. Your friends, spilling your idiot plan."

His brows furrow.

"Stop looking at me like I'm some insane lady yelling the gospel while masturbating on the subway."

"I'd love to, but you did come in yelling with no discernible reason."

I roll my eyes. "I know that you are counting on StarPlay to pick Nephilim over us. I was walking past the game room and heard John saying that you're not planning to put any effort into establishing a collaboration with us because you know that you have the better chance to get the project and—hey?" Jesse stalks to the door, and I whirl around. "Stop!"

He doesn't. His step doesn't falter—at least, until I reach out to grasp the back of his shirt.

He spins to face me. "What are you doing?"

I let go of the fabric like it's a pot of boiling water, a little embarrassed. "Are you just . . . going?"

"Yes. I have something to do."

"You can't just *leave* in the middle of a conversation."

"Is there a law against it?" He looks down at me with a narrow-eyed expression that broadcasts impatience. Aside from the mistletoe, it's the most emotion he's ever shown toward me, and something within me that somehow managed to survive the stress and weight of his indifference for years finally *cracks*. "You know, Jesse, I'm not radioactive. At my last checkup I didn't test positive for any contagious diseases. I regularly brush my teeth, I'm not trying to get anyone to invest in cryptocurrency, I use both deodorant *and* antiperspirant, I never give people unsolicited Netflix recommendations—"

"Are you done?" His arms cross on a chest that's just too broad, and . . .

Yes. I *could* be done. But now that Jesse Andrews is standing in front of me and actually *listening*, I find that there's more I'd like to talk about.

"Did I do something to you?" The question slips out of me quietly, a little subdued. It surprises me—and Jesse, too, judging from how his eyes widen.

"No, you haven't." His tone is lower, too. "What are you talking about?"

"Right. Because, I mean, maybe you don't like me, and that's fair and your prerogative, whatever. But you always act like you wish I wasn't around, and I *know* I'm not just being paranoid because I heard you back at the engagement party, and . . ."

Laughter rolls in through the closed door. A few people are walking in the hallway, and by this point I easily recognize the voices' owners: Ashley, and John, and—

Jesse spins on his heels to go after them, but I can't let him leave now that I have some hope of figuring out the reason behind this weirdly tense dynamic we've developed. Without conscious thought, I grab at him again. This time my hand meets his arm, and my fingers close around his wrist as I pull him back to me. "Jesse, can we please—"

With no apparent effort, he yanks his arm free of my grip and takes one step back, increasing the distance between us. He rubs his wrist, as if scarred by my touch. When he finally looks at my face his cheekbones are dusted with red, his jaw is clenched, and his eyes are blazing with—something.

His breath comes a little quickly. For unknown reasons, so does mine.

"I'm sorry." My face burns hot. "I didn't mean to—I wasn't . . ."

My jaw drops open as he turns to exit the room, leaving me in the middle of the library to wonder what the hell just happened. I exhale slowly, rub my eyes with my thumb and index finger, let my arm drop to my side.

And that's when I notice it.

On the chair Jesse vacated, still open facedown, is an old hardcover book. It's clearly a well-loved copy, the corners scuffed by constant use, full of earmarked pages and tabs.

The Sunken Heart, the cover says. *The Limerence Saga, Volume 1.*

Chapter 6

THE FOLLOWING MORNING, BEFORE I MAKE MY WAY DOWN-stairs for breakfast, I have to actively beg my forehead to quit scowling.

This will be fine, I promise it when its muscles won't re-lax. *We'll figure it out.*

But I'm not so sure. My room is cold—and *stays* cold, no matter how much I dial up the heat. I spent all night tossing and turning, my thoughts a jittery jumble of resentment, disappointment, anger, and the heavy, disconsolate fear that my chance at working on the Limerence IP is becoming slimmer by the minute. Because what John said was true: If it comes down to us vs. Nephilim, StarPlay will choose the more well-rounded option.

And that's *not* us.

Can we talk? I texted Mike around three a.m. **Alone. Lead Designer to CEO.**

His reply came first thing this morning. **Of course. After breakfast? Are you going to be skiing?**

Nope, I value the integrity of my skull bones.

What a coincidence, so do I. Let's chat then.

I sit on the bed, dejected, and hear Jesse move about his room. The wood creaks, his steps vibrate through the wall, and he feels oddly . . . close. Solid and present and *real*.

I hate him. Him, and his plan, and the disconcerted face he made when I touched him, like I'm an intruder in his life. I hate being around him, and I want to stab him with an emery board. Clearly, he's terrible both for my self-respect and my criminal record.

The first thing I notice when I make my way inside the dining room is that last night's place card trial has been discontinued. Nephilim and FlyButter are split with a surgical precision that reminds me of boys and girls in an eighth-grade sex education class.

I dispassionately grab a blueberry muffin and a cup of

hot chocolate, then take a seat next to Shannon, who sports the joyous but tired expression of someone who's been having illegal amounts of clandestine sex.

A few seats to the right, I spot Jesse eating a small plate of eggs. He shovels food in his mouth with ruthless efficiency, not quite taking part in the conversations floating around him. The glasses are back, and I notice the silliest details, like how perfectly they sit on his nose, or the way the stems disappear into the small curls at his temples.

"You okay?" Shannon asks me.

"Yeah. I just . . ."

Do I tell her? About what I overheard last night?

No. No, I don't. Because if FlyButter people find out, they'll take it as the perfect excuse to openly declare war on Nephilim. And even though an argument could be made that the Nephilim team fully deserves to have their cars keyed—or, let's be honest, *burned*—I woke up with a single conviction.

I *want* to work on *Limerence 3*. I *want* to put my spin on that game. I *want* to hear about kids playing it with their dads. I want to be able to think about how much mine would have enjoyed doing the same with me. And since I can't imagine any scenario in which open warfare between the two studios will lead to me being involved in its design, I . . .

My train of thought stumbles, then halts as I watch Jesse down what's left of his orange juice and stand. Other men might require some throat clearing to get a room's attention, but not *this* guy. Everyone instantly falls silent, looking up at the dark expression that seems to match the way I feel.

"I'm going to cut to the chase," he says, arms crossed on his chest like a nightclub bouncer. He sounds . . . I don't know. Angry? Scary? No trace of the affable calm he usually displays when he talks to . . . well, to people who are not *me*. I shudder at his tone, and when I look around, most people seem just as alarmed.

"I have no authority over anyone at FlyButter. But I am the lead designer at Nephilim, and as you all know, I oversaw the *Limerence 3* project proposal. What I am about to say is exclusively for my team, but I'll do this once, publicly, so that *everyone* in this lodge understands where I stand."

Most insecure public speakers—and I know this because I *am* one—tend to find a safe audience member and let their gaze settle on them. Not Jesse, though. His eyes meet everyone's in the most inescapable way, as though daring us to drift off, or push back. When it's clear that no one would be foolish enough to do that, his cold, cold stare lands on John.

"I've had this conversation with a couple of you already, in private. But I'm not sure who was reached by the bullshit that came to my attention yesterday, so let me make something very clear."

A pause. No one seems to breathe.

"This retreat is *not* a waste of time. Its purpose is *not* to annoy FlyButter into pulling back from the project, and if that's the impression under which you came here, you are invited to return home and leave the project. I acknowledge that there have been issues between our studios in the past, but the goal is to move past them. If you're not willing to do that, you know where the door is."

He waits before continuing, as if to give people the opportunity to leave. I wonder if he understands that we're all paralyzed by . . . by him.

"Here is what some of you don't seem to grasp: Both FlyButter and Nephilim are midsized indie studios. Neither team has the capabilities to undertake a project the size of *Limerence 3* and meet StarPlay's vision *alone*. There are larger studios who are ready to swoop in if we fuck this up, so let me make it clear: This is not an us-*or*-them situation. It's an us-*and*-them, or someone else altogether. And let me disclose something personal: I want to work on this game. And if I catch any of you doing anything that stands between me and what I want, I *will* address it. *Swiftly*."

I shudder at the threat in his tone, and as I do, my view of Jesse Andrews and his role in this industry reorients. I always respected his work, but after what happened a year ago I couldn't help seeing him as something of an enemy. And yet, right now he's my ally—my strongest one, perhaps.

Maybe that's why, in a spur-of-the-moment decision that

shocks even *me*, I stand. "As the lead designer of FlyButter," I say, letting my tone absorb the same uncompromising hardness that I use when my niece tries to cheat at Uno, "everything Jesse said goes for me, too."

I notice Mila's slightly befuddled look. Ethan's eyebrows shoot up. Kai's scowl seems slightly betrayed, but I don't care. They don't love Limerence as much as I do.

"And I'll go further," I continue. "The goal is not just being assigned to the project and pocketing the funds. The goal is to make the best possible version of this game, and we can only do it together. If there are legitimate interpersonal issues between members of the two teams, please come to me and I'll help deal with them. But if I hear anyone making snide remarks, being needlessly antagonistic, or generally creating a hostile work environment . . ." I trail off, because . . . what? What will I do? It's not like I have the power to fire people without Mike's approval—

"You *will* be fired," Mike says, standing abruptly.

I'm so relieved, I could kiss him. Even though this whole thing *is* taking a turn for the "Oh Captain! My Captain!" very quickly.

"Let it be clear," he continues, "that I stand behind everything that was said. If you're not a team player, there's no point in having you on the team."

A brief moment of silence follows, in which every gaze drifts toward Otto. He is, after all, CEO of Nephilim. We need him to back us up, and he seems to be aware. Because he stands with a resigned sigh, faces his people, and says, "If you fuck this up for me—If I catch any of you provoking fights, bickering, or being generally annoying, you're not just fired, you're *blacklisted*. I have shit to do. Do not waste my time. As usual, what Jesse says, goes."

Mike stares at Otto like he's a knight in shining armor who took off a helmet to sensually shake his luscious ginger hair. It's a minute before he can tear his eyes away. "Right." He clears his throat. "So . . . Does anyone have anything they'd like to say about this matter?"

Silence.

"John?" Jesse interjects. Still cross-armed. Still hardass. "Any comments?"

"No," John croaks.

I study the way every single head across the teams shakes energetically, as though we've never been in anything but agreement, as though the idea of scattering pushpins in each other's beds never occurred to any of us.

For the first time since I got here, the smile stretching my lips is heartfelt, and I think to myself, *Now we're cooking.*

Chapter 7

I'M RELUCTANTLY ALLOWING MYSELF TO HOPE THAT THINGS might turn out all right.

Our impromptu motivational-speech-slash-threatening-ultimatum may have taken everyone by surprise, and may very well be followed by an hour or two of eggshell-walking and suspicious tiptoeing around each other, but with some advanced teeth-pulling we can manage to move past that.

"I need your help," I tell Ethan and Shannon when they corner me after breakfast to ask if I've been body-snatched by yetis. "Please, will you two try to break the ice and interact with some of the Nephilim people you don't hate? Do it for me. I'll clean the microwave in the lounge for the next month."

"Three months," Ethan rebuts.

I give him a level look. "How about one week, *and* I don't tell Mike to fire you?"

He bows his head to hide a smile. "Your wish is my command, my liege."

And they do what I asked.

A little later, I see them heading for the double black diamond slopes with Otto, Jesse, and a handful of other people, and blow Ethan a kiss. He pretends to catch it and put it in his pocket, which has Shannon shaking her head in amusement and Jesse averting his gaze.

Our corniness is clearly too cringe for him to bear, and I can't blame him.

I never planned on venturing out of the lodge, but when Clara and another Nephilim engineer ask if I want to join them on one of the easier slopes, I seize their offer of friendship. We spend the morning snowplowing our way down a practically horizontal surface, four adults surrounded by a bunch of eight-year-olds. It doesn't really embody my preconceived idea of a "good time," but I discover that I actually enjoy being terrible at shit with people who are just as terrible at the same shit. In the afternoon, I curl up in front of the fireplace on the mezzanine with *The Sunken Heart*, trying not to wonder about its twin copy, the one also vacationing under this very roof.

It's my seventh reread of the book in as many months. In

fact, I've now gone through the entire series so many times, I could probably recite it by heart. That's not because I enjoy the story and adore revisiting characters—though I do. The problem is, I cannot shake the feeling that I'm overlooking something. I'm very proud of the ideas I presented to StarPlay for *Limerence 3*, and I know that I'm the right person to design the game. Still, I can do better. Because at this moment, something isn't right.

What matters most to me is Aqualuna. I want the game to celebrate her strength. I want to show how formidable and independent and resilient she is. I want her love for adventure to inspire others as much as it inspires me. And yet, I feel like something about her eludes me—like the version of her I proposed falls flat. The Aqualuna I created for the game lacks a quality that book Aqualuna has in heaps, but I can't point my finger on what is missing, and I need to figure it out before production starts.

So, I spend the afternoon rereading. *Again.* I drink approximately three gallons of hot chocolate, smiling as I study the little star-shaped marshmallows floating around the surface of my mug.

By the time the black diamond slope contingent returns, the sun is setting. I lift my head from the book the moment I hear them come in, and when I peek from the mezzanine, I'm relieved to see them laughing and joking with one another as they hang their skis on the rack.

Later that night, after a delightfully uneventful dinner, a few of us take over one of the multimedia rooms and marathon holiday Hallmark movies while snacking on popcorn.

"Jesus," Kai complains after taking a handful of mine. "Why don't you just go ahead and eat a stick of salted butter?"

"I could," I answer while chewing. "But the popcorn makes it easier to pick up."

I head for bed before the third film begins, and Mike joins me, yawning. We're in the middle of an animated argument over whether sphynx cats are cute beyond belief (me) or elephant-eared, horrifying wrinkly goblins (Mike), when Ashley comes running toward us.

Her steps are wobbly, and her eyes pleading. "Thank god you guys are here. Please help me?"

Mike and I exchange a baffled look. Judging from the way Ashley's swaying on her feet, though, I doubt she's in a position to notice.

"Are you okay?" Mike asks. "Do you maybe need a glass of water . . ." He falls silent as we follow her into a nearby room.

It's one of the smaller dens, equipped only with a TV, a couch, and a couple of chairs, but she's not watching a movie. I immediately recognize the cowboy graphics on the screen and grin. "Are you playing *Red Dead Redemption 2*? It's my favorite—oh."

At first, all I notice is the hair peeping from the back of the couch, the chuff of orange-red so distinctive, it could belong to only Otto. Then I spot the second, darker mop of hair right next to it, and the PlayStation that has been hooked up to the LED TV.

I walk around the couch, half expecting to find Jesse and Otto passed out. They are, in fact, conscious, and very busy playing a grotesquely lethargic game of tag. It mainly consists of staying put and poking each other's arms at alternating intervals. Occasionally, they crack themselves up. And they are too engrossed in the activity to pay attention to me or Mike.

"What happened?" I whisper. Then my eyes fall onto the three open bottles on the coffee table, and the question seems silly. There's quite a bit missing from each one. I bend closer to read the labels: Vodka, vermouth, and something I've never heard of before called "sambuca." "That's a lot of alcohol."

"It's my fault," Ashley says, leaning against the wall for support. "We played a drinking game."

"What game?"

"Take a shot whenever Dutch calls someone 'son.'"

I gasp out a laugh. "That's *a lot* of shots."

"Yup."

"You seem to be doing much better than them," Mike points out.

"Yeah. That's because I always cheat and stop drinking much earlier than they do. But they're already drunk, so they barely realize."

Mike and I exchange another glance—him, a bit judgmental, and me, admiring her cunning.

"Do they, um . . ." Mike scratches his chin. "Do they need medical attention?"

"Oh my god, no. We do this *all the time*."

"You play *Red Dead Redemption 2* drinking games all the time," I repeat skeptically, leaning on the wall.

"Of course. You don't?"

"Can't say I do."

She waves a dismissive hand, like I'm speaking nonsense. "Whatever. The next step for them is usually falling asleep wherever they are, so . . . Can you help me carry them back to their rooms?"

Mike frowns. "Um, yeah. But are you sure that—"

"Thanks!" Ashley leans forward to hug him and press a kiss on his cheek. "You're the best. Good night!"

We watch her skip out of the room, her pace decidedly steadier than before. "I don't think I like her," Mike mutters.

"I don't think she gives a shit." I sigh, and we both step in front of the couch, studying the scene with hands on our hips. The sleeping part of their night seems to have commenced. The frequency of the tags has decreased to null, and Jesse and Otto are sprawled backward, their heads tilted back on the tops of the cushions. Their eyes are closed. "Do you think they're crashing out?" I ask. "And, as a follow-up question: I know we recently brokered a peace-keeping agreement with Nephilim, but would it be in bad taste to take very compromising pictures of them and disseminate them on the internet—"

"He's so fucking cute," Mike interrupts, clearly not listening to a word I'm saying. I follow the direction of his eyes and realize that he's looking at Otto. Otto, whose mouth hangs open, and has visibly drooled on his sweatshirt. There is also something that looks like boogers on his right cheek, but who knows? It could be a wart.

"So Otto's cute, but sphynx cats aren't?" I mumble in disbelief, but Mike seems determined to ignore me to engage in other, more interesting activities—namely, lovingly pushing Otto's hair back from his forehead. Jesus. "Dude. For real? How many times did you guys get together and break up?"

"Only like, five or six. Seven if you count the night at GameCon when—"

"You know what, no need for detail. It was a rhetorical question."

"Yeah," Mike agrees. "We have no time. We gotta take them to bed."

I snort—and then realize that he's not joking. "What? Why?"

"Because."

"Because, why? There's heat in here. It's just us staying at the lodge, so it's not like they'll be robbed or kidnapped and sold into sex slavery. We could find a couple of blankets and . . ."

I must be talking a bit too loudly. Otto doesn't stir, but Jesse's dark eyes slowly blink open. He tries to straighten, and several curls fall on his forehead, somehow creating a perfect image of sophisticated chaos. How does he manage to look like a nerd who's also an athlete who's also a *poet*?

"Viola," he says—slurs, really, voice deep and gravelly.

I sigh. "Yup. Me."

He mumbles something else, something that sounds like *good dream*, but I cannot make out any more of it. His full lips are slightly parted, and there's something almost peaceful about the way he stares at me. His usually sharp eyes seem glassy, confused, but his cheeks are such a pretty red, they remind me of our encounter last night.

I want to touch them. See if they radiate heat as much as I expect.

"Viola's going to take you to your room," Mike says, bending to wrap Otto's arm around his neck. "Okay, Jesse?"

Jesse nods with the cogency of a sloth who just woke up from a twenty-five-year sleep, and I'm speechless long enough for Mike to lift up Otto and get him halfway to the door. "Wait a minute," I say. "Otto weighs half as much as Jesse. And I weigh less than you, so it would make more sense for me to—"

"Make sure you put a bucket or something similar next to his bed," he yells before turning the corner. "In case he gets sick."

The room falls silent, and I stand there alone, like the fool I am.

Or—not quite alone.

My eyes drift to Jesse, who seems to have fallen back asleep, this time with his head hanging forward.

"Shit," I mutter.

He is, at least, a more graceful drunk than Otto. No boogers, or drool. I debate the pros and cons of leaving him here to stew in his own ethanol, and in the end, the deciding factor is simply that for all the years of *weirdness* between us, what he did this morning might have saved my Limerence dreams.

"Hey," I say. When there's no response I begin to poke at his biceps. Which, admittedly, does feel like the biceps of someone who does triathlons and has opinions on lactic acid. "Can you—Jesse? Can you wake up?"

He lifts his head with effort. Good enough, I guess.

"You fell asleep on the couch, so I'm going to take you upstairs to your room, 'kay? Can you walk a bit? I can help you balance, but you're heavy and—"

"Viola," he says again, this time sounding breathless. For whatever reason, his tone makes my cheeks heat.

Honestly, he might be better drunk than sober. Some people become aggressive when they overindulge, but Jesse is docile, and once I figure out how to leverage his arm over my shoulders, the process of dragging him to bed works smoothly.

I try not to think too hard about the previous day, and his expression when my hand closed around his wrist. I don't think he likes to be touched. *Technically, though, you're only touching him through his sweater*, I think as I coax him upstairs, feeling his heat as he leans against my side. This might be our most pleasant interaction to date, and yes, it counts even if Jesse is mostly unconscious.

The layout of his room is exactly like mine—a huge four-poster bed, large windows that lead to a balcony, and a sitting area with a small round table and two chairs. I find that I'm not surprised to discover he's a bit of a neat freak, with the result that unlike my room, his doesn't look like a hurricane ran through it.

"Two more steps and we're on the bed," I tell him, a little out of breath from supporting his weight. Jesse hums agreeably, and when his thigh hits the mattress, he lets himself fall back faceup. His curls, just a little too long, bounce on the pillow. I take off his shoes and lift his legs onto the bedspread.

"You owe me big-time," I say, though he won't remember any of this.

I move the trash can closer to the bed, then turn on the bedside lamp and make to head out. I'm feeling like I'm really paying it forward tonight, when a hand closes around my wrist. It startles me, and I trip on the plush carpet, losing my balance and planting my ass on the edge of the bed.

"Shit, I—"

Jesse's fingers are warm and steady against my skin, his grip strong enough to anchor me. Sloshed as he is, I could wriggle free with little effort, but when I look down I find him staring up at me with a peaceful, contemplative expression that gives me pause.

"Are you . . . do you need anything? I can get you some water if you . . ." My voice trails off as he lets go of my wrist. My skin feels cold, as if already missing his touch, though maybe that's not it. Maybe it's the backs of his fingers inching up my bare arm that make me shiver, slow and light and purposeful until they reach my shoulder and abruptly—stop.

"You," he says, and I find it odd that all of a sudden his voice sounds remarkably sober. "You are the most beautiful thing I've ever seen."

A wave of heat creeps up my chest. I snort out a nervous laugh to stifle it. "You must have me mixed up with someone else—"

Jesse's hand moves up, from my shoulder to my chin, and

just like that I can feel the warmth of his skin again. His thumb comes to rest on my lips, lingers there, and . . . I can hardly continue talking with his finger over my mouth.

"Viola," he whispers.

Time becomes thicker. Slower. There is no more air in the space between us, and a storm blows up in my rib cage. Jesse's thumb swipes back and forth over my lower lip, something wistful and yearning and hungry in his stare that I cannot quite comprehend. Until his mouth twitches in a sad half smile, and he says:

"I haven't thought about anything but you since the first time I saw you."

With that, Jesse's eyes blink closed, his hand drops back to his side, and he falls into a deep sleep.

Chapter 8

I MOST DEFINITELY DO *NOT* STARE AT MY CEILING FOR HOURS thinking about what happened.

Not at all.

And if I do, it's probably just all the hot chocolate I guzzled throughout the day—it contains caffeine, a three a.m. Google search informs me. Or maybe it's the cold of the room, which has seeped into my bone marrow and seems to have become part of my body, despite the blankets and the fires and the layers of clothes I've been putting on.

It has *nothing* to do with Jesse, who surely did *not* mean what he said. He was drunk. He was half asleep. He was out of his mind.

But he said your name, a little voice whispers in my ear. *Viola.* With the same precise, specific tone he might use to inform me that the current patch of my game is a bug fest and has caused considerable slowdown issues. He said, "*Viola,*" and he looked at me, and then he touched me. Like *that. He said that you were beautiful.*

He also ignored you for five years and declared that he wanted nothing to do with you, a more sensible, less sultry voice suggests. It definitely has a point.

I end up falling asleep in the early hours of the morning and wake up late, groggy and anxious. Outside my window the snow is falling, big, silent flakes that look like they'll stick to the ground, even to my meteorologically inexperienced eyes. I wonder whether fresh precipitation will cause more people to stay in and off the slopes. Then I check my texts, find Mike's message, and realize that the person I'm most interested in avoiding won't be skiing anyway.

Let's have a meeting in the early afternoon—Otto, Jesse, you, and me. We can make sure we're on the same page when it comes to Limerence 3 and present a united front to the team in case they have questions.

I close my eyes and sit on the side of the bed until I'm shivering.

Breakfast is no longer being served by the time I get to the dining room, so I make do with cold coffee, a slightly stale bagel, and some suspicious-looking grape jelly. I'm alone at the table when Ethan comes in and takes a seat in front of me. He glances furtively around, like he's afraid of being followed, then leans in to whisper:

"We need to talk."

I blink, putting down what's left of my breakfast. It's gross, anyway. "Okay."

"It's a bit of a delicate matter."

"Um. Okay?" I hesitate. Ethan is usually more direct than this. It's why I like him. "Is this about Shannon?"

"No. Well," he amends with a tilt of his head, "yes. Partially. Indirectly."

Oh, god. This can't possibly be good. "Okay. Just as a warning, if it has anything to do with your sex life I might not be the best person to ask advice of, because I don't think I want the mental image of you and Shannon doing stuff that involves, I don't know, feet or handcuffs or—"

"Have you been telling people that we're dating?" he asks, sounding dead serious.

"What? No. I know you and Shannon have decided to keep it a secret, and—

"No, I meant . . . You and I. Have you told anyone that *you and I* are dating?"

Whatever I expected, this was *not* it. "What?"

He rubs his jaw with his palm. "Okay, I know this is going to sound ridiculous, but—there are people who think that you're my girlfriend. And that I'm your boyfriend. And like . . . I know sometimes we say that you're my work wife and joke about that kind of stuff because of all the late nights at the office, but I wanted to make sure that—"

"What—who? Who thinks that?"

"Well, judging from the way he cornered me against a wall, Jesse Andrews does."

I open my mouth to answer, but no sound comes out for the longest time. When it finally does, my voice is little more than a croak. "Why . . . Why would he do that?"

Ethan shrugs. "He saw Shannon and me holding hands. And maybe even kiss? Earlier this morning we went for a walk, and then we came back in and we thought we were alone and—then Shannon went back to her room to shower and—" He rubs the back of his neck, clearly upset. "I'd never seen Jesse like that. I've always thought he was an easygoing guy—I mean, we were skiing together yesterday and having a hell of a good time, so . . ."

My mouth is agape. "But . . . what does this have to do with me being—or not being—your girlfriend?"

"That's the thing. Once he had me alone in one of the rooms and scowled so hard I thought I might shit myself, he said, and I'm basically quoting, that if I am the kind of piece of shit who will cheat on his partner while she's sleeping under the same roof, I could at least make a better effort to avoid being caught. And then he reminded me that you were upstairs and could have walked down any minute, and how hurt you'd be, and—"

"What the hell?" I almost yell, and Ethan frantically shushes me down.

"Hey, let's keep this quiet."

I'm too astonished by what he's saying to point out that we're alone. I lean toward him over the table and whisper, "I have never said or implied that you and I are dating. Least of all to Jesse. I have barely ever had a conversation with him."

You did last night, the little voice murmurs. *And the one before.*

Yeah, the wiser voice replies harshly. *And look how those clusterfucks turned out.*

"Right, I thought so. I mean—I'm not sure why I'm asking. I know you wouldn't." Ethan shrugs. "Jesse must have assumed. I mean, you and I *do* tend to be attached at the hip during conventions, but that's because you have impeccable taste in choosing which panels to attend."

I shoot him a small grin. "Likewise." Ethan is right.

Jesse must have *assumed*, heavy on the *ass*, because of circumstantial evidence. It's the only acceptable explanation.

Or it would be, if it didn't require a level of attention to my habits that I cannot imagine Jesse sparing. He's not interested enough in me to even *wonder* about my dating life.

Or at least, that's what I believed until last night.

"I haven't thought about anything but you since the first time I saw you."

"Glad we figured this out." Ethan looks relieved. "I wouldn't have pegged Jesse as that type, you know?"

"What type?"

"The type to threaten me because he thought I was cheating on a girl that he barely knows. Seems a bit too . . . caveman?"

"Caveman," I repeat.

"Yeah. That überprotective shit, when he practically ordered me to come clean with you? Not on brand *at all*."

"Right," I say weakly. My mind is spinning in an odd way, making me dizzy.

"You are the most beautiful thing I've ever seen."

"I ended up telling him, by the way," Ethan adds. "No other way around it."

"Telling him what?" I ask.

"That we're not dating. That Shannon and I have been sexing each other up for weeks and I'm in love with her. Isn't it weird that I told Jesse Andrews before I told Shannon?"

Ethan shakes his head, amused. "But it's true. I don't think I had admitted it to myself, either, before, but Jesse is so damn tall and he looked pissed and I did not want to risk it, and . . . I don't know, maybe it's a good thing that he did that. The panic made a few things clearer for me, you know?"

"What did he . . ." My mouth is as dry as the desert. I have to swallow before continuing. "What did he say? When you told him?"

"Nothing. Nothing, he apologized and then he left. He looked . . . kind of dumbstruck, to be honest. Like I told him that Santa and leprechauns don't really exist?"

I sag against the back of my chair. Ethan moves on to a tangentially related topic, some Irish leprechaun game he came across the other day that's "so fucking bonkers," I absolutely need to play it, but I'm no longer paying attention.

Because all I can think of is Jesse's voice when he said, "*Viola*."

■ ■ ■ ■ ■

AFTER MY CONVERSATION WITH ETHAN, I LOOK FOR JESSE ALL over the lodge, but he's nowhere to be found. I'm convinced that he's avoiding me. When the time of our meeting comes, I'm so certain he won't show up that I physically recoil when I see him already sitting at the pale oak table.

"Did you see a spider or something?" Otto asks me in his

usual sneering tone—which, I'm starting to understand, is his *only* tone. How unfortunate, for him *and* for the rest of us.

"No," I say. "No."

Mike points at the chair next to him. "Sit down, Vee."

Jesse is across from me, calmly sipping from a steaming mug of pitch-black coffee. I watch him suspiciously, willing him to meet my eyes, but even when he does, his gaze is inscrutable. Nothing in his behavior, demeanor, or tone indicates that a few hours ago he nearly held Ethan's head over a toilet because he suspected him of cheating on me.

Fascinating, I think, as he starts the meeting by pulling up a few designs on his tablet and introducing some of his ideas on how to best adapt aspects of the Limerence stories into different levels, quests, tools, characters. It's clear that Otto is *very* hands-off—a money and logistics figure rather than the creative force behind the games produced by Nephilim—and the more I listen to Jesse, the gladder I become for it.

Because Jesse Andrews absolutely *gets* it.

Limerence 1 and *2* were good games peppered with moments of greatness, but they had several limitations, first among them the fact that they used the world-building and the magic system of the books to create completely new stories with new casts of characters. Jesse, like me, has no intention of doing that, and plans to stick much closer to the source material.

The knowledge makes my heart pound faster.

I need to talk to you, I think at him. *Alone. Right now. I need to ask you . . . so many questions.*

"Four acts might be overambitious," Jesse says, "but I don't think StarPlay would object to shooting for the moon."

"Are you dead set on two playable characters?" Mike asks, frowning.

Jesse nods. "It's the best option."

"And they would be the warlock and the human, right?"

"Correct."

"Hang on." I raise my finger to stop him. "In your proposal, you wanted both Aqualuna and Noham to be playable?"

"You didn't?" Jesse seems as surprised as I am.

"Well . . . The saga is from Aqualuna's point of view."

He nods. "And?"

"And . . ." I fall quiet.

And? I ask myself, leaning back in my chair to think it through. I always conceptualized Limerence as primarily Aqualuna's story, and I still think it is. But that's not to say that Noham doesn't have his own arc in the books. We may never be directly in his head, but he and Aqualuna have so many long talks, they share such a large amount of space on the page, he's just as much the protagonist as she is.

But having him as a playable character would completely change the narrative structure. It would require—

"I don't know." Otto's voice cuts through my thoughts.

"We could make it so much easier on ourselves if we only had one playable character."

"Yeah," Mike agrees. "To be frank, Noham's role is so complicated, it would be a pain to adapt him even as a non-playable character. We could cut him out altogether and give the girl other sidekicks, maybe from the first two games—"

"No," I say.

As quickly and firmly as Jesse does.

Mike glances between us, a hint of betrayal in his eyes, as though we're unjustly ganging up against him. "Fine." He shrugs. "If you prefer, we could cut Aqualuna and have Noham as the—"

"No," we say in unison, so vehemently that Mike shrinks back in his chair.

"What's wrong with you two?"

I scoff. "What's wrong with *us*?"

Mike frowns. "It's not like you were planning to have Noham as a playable character all along, Viola."

"No, but I would never dream of cutting him *or* Aqualuna out."

"Listen, I'm just trying to be pragmatic."

"Have you read the books?" Jesse, usually congenial, sounds as full of contempt as I feel.

"I . . . yes. A while ago. I was going to reread them, but only got through the first three. Or, um, two and a half, and—they are very *verbose*."

Jesse sighs, broadcasting my exact feelings. "Without Noham or Aqualuna—without Noham *and* Aqualuna together—there is no story," he says firmly. "Which is what the first two games never understood, and the reason we need a third. The titular limerence is theirs. What makes this series special are not the monsters and spells, but the relationship between the two main characters. If we lose them, we lose the spirit of the material. We may as well turn around and adapt something else, or design a game from scratch."

Mike cocks his head. "That seems like an exaggeration."

Jesse's eyes narrow. "Do you know what 'limerence' means?"

"I can't say I do."

"It's unrequited love. The act of desiring someone you can never have. Ever experienced that?"

Mike flushes.

Otto looks away.

And I . . . I find myself continuing Jesse's thought. "Throughout the series, Noham and Aqualuna have adventures together. They start out as begrudging allies, then become friends, then fall in love. Most readers think that the story is leading them toward a happy ever after, but in the last chapter of the fifth book we discover who they *really* are."

"And that is?" Otto asks.

"Reincarnated lovers. Who have spent countless lifetimes together, but are destined to eternal misery. They have been cursed for the misdeeds of their ancestors. Every time they are reborn, only one of them will be able to recall their previous lives. That person is burdened with the knowledge that the moment the other confesses their love, they will instantly die."

Jesse nods. His eyes hold the same faint trace of surprise I'm feeling. It's like we're both thinking: *You, too? You love these books as much as I do? You understand, don't you?*

"In the series," Jesse explains, "Noham recognizes Aqualuna as his one true love the second they meet. But he knows about the curse, and is aware that the moment she professes her love, she will remember their past lives. He will die, and she will be alone for what is left of her life."

"And *that*," I continue, "will kick off a new cycle. In the next life, Aqualuna will be the one with magic powers, and Noham will be human, and he'll only remember their previous encounters when he professes *his* love—and she dies."

Otto grimaces. "Jesus, this is fucking depressing."

"It's not," Jesse says simply. His eyes meet mine for a split second that makes my lungs empty of all air. It ends so quickly, I wonder whether I imagined it, and when I try to search his face he's once again looking down at his tablet, pulling out a diagram about level structure that means moving on from what we're discussing. And yet he adds, lower, as if not meant for anyone's ears, "It's an ode to the enduring power of love. To wanting, and to the way the feeling can survive for the longest time. Even without having."

Chapter 9

AFTER THE MEETING IS OVER I'M DYING TO TALK TO JESSE alone, but Mike—gifted with the excellent timing of a finance bro who buys a bunch of stocks the day before a market crash—asks me to help him pick a gift from his cousin's wedding registry. When we're done scrolling through miles and miles of towel pictures, I look around, but Jesse is gone, and . . .

No, dammit.

I run toward my room, darting right past Kai, Manny, and Mila, all wrapped in winter coats and thick hats and ski gloves.

"Oh, Vee, you're here! We're going to take a walk in the

snow since the storm doesn't seem to be too intense, do you want to join—"

"No time," I reply, rushing upstairs.

Once I'm standing in front of Jesse's room, I don't hesitate. I knock, no doubt more forcefully than necessary, and square my shoulders as I hear him taking the few steps to the door. His eyes widen once he sees me, but only for a second. Then his expression shuts off into something impenetrably pleasant.

"Hi. How can I help you?"

I duck under the arm that holds the door open, step inside the bedroom, and go to stand in the middle of it. When I turn, his brow is furrowed in confusion. "What are you doing?" he asks.

"Will you close the door, please?"

He huffs out a single, baffled laugh. "Is this something you do often? Walk into someone's room and start making demands of them?"

"Suit yourself, then." I take a deep breath, wet my lips, and come right out with it. "Do you like me?"

He goes still. Absolutely, *utterly* still, like his heart stopped beating and his lungs shut down, and for a handful of seconds I'm a tiny bit worried that I might have broken Jesse Andrews. Or at least severely damaged him. After a while, though, his lips press together, and then he *does* push the door closed behind him.

"See?" I lean back against one of the bed's posts, relief fluttering in my stomach. I hope I look braver than I feel. "I figured you might want to have some privacy for this one."

"You did, didn't you."

His tone is dry, and it feels a bit like he's punting, trying to buy time, so I ask again, "Do you like me?"

He looks very calm, but he's not. I *know* it in my bones. "Why would you think that?"

"Because you told me. Last night." He blinks, confused. "Ever wonder how you got from *Red Dead Redemption* to bed?" I point a thumb at my chest. "This girl. You weigh a ton, by the way."

His eyes widen, this time in worry. "Did I touch you? If I did anything that you—"

"No, nothing like that. But you *did* confess to . . ." I shrug. I don't think I have the vocabulary for this. "Having a thing for me, for lack of a better term. I figured you were just wasted, but then I found out that this morning you assaulted Ethan for supposedly 'cheating' on me—"

"I did *not* assault him."

"Whatever. Semantics."

Jesse rolls his eyes, crossing his arms over his chest. "Is he always that dramatic?"

"Yup."

"I barely talked to him."

I wave an impatient hand and continue, trying to sound

calm and rational even though I feel anything but. "The thing is, ever since we met you've been so doggedly indifferent to me that if twenty-four hours ago someone had asked whether you were interested in me, I'd have laughed in their face. And I'm not even gonna get into the mistletoe incident, and the fact that you told my cousin that you wanted nothing to do with me. Because yes, I did hear that. But then last night you mentioned something about . . ." I cannot bring myself to say, *About me, being beautiful. About wanting me.* So I continue with, "About the way I look. And this morning you threatened my friend—yep, he's just a good friend, always has been—and, well, I hope you will forgive me for coming across as conceited, but I think you can understand why I cannot help but wonder if you . . ." I pause, holding his eyes for a beat, ". . . like me."

In the end, I don't need an answer. Not a verbal one, for sure. Not with the way Jesse looks at me, his eyes dark and clear and for once so, *so* easy to read. This man might hide and deflect and withdraw, but he's no liar. And the truth is there on his face, for me to pick up and study and marvel at.

"Right," I mumble. My voice sounds strange and croaky to my own ears. "I thought so."

He closes his eyes, running a hand through his hair. My brain registers the movement, and all I can think of is how soft the curls look. "Viola, I . . ."

He. He . . . *something.* As time trickles by, the silence in the room broken only by the laughter of the people exploring the woods outside, it becomes clear that Jesse has no intention of completing the sentence.

But at this point, I just want to understand.

"Why, then?" I turn around and walk to the window, taking in branches of pine trees that look about to collapse under the weight of the snow. "Is it a recent development? It must be." I'm thinking out loud now. Brainstorming possibilities. "Otherwise, why would you go out of your way to avoid me for years? Why would you act so appalled at the idea of kissing me?"

Next to one of the decks, Kai crouches to make a snowball. Shannon beats him to it and slides a handful of ice down his collar. They both scream while Mila takes a video of them with her cell phone.

"Unless," I muse. The thought occurring to me is almost too painful to put in words. "Unless you hate it. Unless you despise yourself for it. Unless your opinion of me is so . . . so low, you're so upset by the idea of being attracted to me, that you just can't help being a total—"

"No."

I turn around. Jesse's face seems so familiar, and yet so new.

"No. I don't . . ." He tiredly runs a hand down his face. "I think the world of you, Viola."

It's hard to believe. Impossible. This whole situation, it's like the script of a bad movie. "Do you really?"

"Yes." Slowly, he nods. And doesn't meet my eyes. "You are . . ." He stops. Touches his lips, as if looking for the right words to describe what I am to him. Which seems to be a whole lot.

"Then why? Why didn't you just . . . try to spend time with me? Try to get to know me? Ask me out?"

Jesse looks to the side, as if fascinated by the framed flower art that looks exactly like the one in my room. The tendons in his neck are suddenly in relief. "That's a little cruel of you to ask, isn't it?"

"Cruel?"

He turns back to me. "You know why I couldn't do any of those things, Viola."

"No, I *don't*. How could I possibly know—"

A knock on the door, and we both jolt. "Housekeeping! May I come in?"

I meet Jesse's eyes again, feeling frustrated by the interruption, but also . . .

No. I *don't* know why he couldn't try to ask me out, especially since I was crushing on him for years. I have no clue, and maybe I should say it to him, I should ask him to come up with a logical explanation for his behavior, or at least with a decent apology. But all at once, I cannot bear to be here, in front of Jesse Andrews—not for a second longer. I scrunch my eyes shut, once, and then step away from the window, giving him as wide a berth as possible as I walk past him.

"None of this matters. We don't need to be anything but coworkers. Let's . . . Let's just pretend that this conversation never happened, okay? We're both good at that. I'll see you around, Jesse."

I open the door and exit the room, flashing the housekeeper a subdued smile. As I hurry down the stairs, I think I hear the sound of my name being called, but I never turn back.

Chapter 10

I REALLY, TRULY DO NOT EXPECT ANYTHING TO CHANGE IN MY relationship with Jesse—at least *not* for the better.

He likes me. Fine. Sure. But clearly has some kind of hang-up about it. And I . . . well, I may have liked him for years, but that ship has sailed and even sunk, about a year ago. I have no intention of putting up a fight against the aforementioned hang-up.

So, that's it. Game over. He and I are going to be colleagues, good colleagues, but I'm determined to not think about him in any nonprofessional capacity for a second longer.

And yet, Jesse might have other ideas.

I get a sense of it the following morning, when I'm precariously balancing food on my plate at the breakfast buffet, wondering if I can fit that banana-walnut muffin on top of my eggs and still reasonably expect that the majestic architectural structure I built won't collapse.

Yes—I hype myself up—*I can do this.*

Except, no. I can't. I realize it on my way back to the table, when the muffin wobbles and slips and begins a tragic, facedown plunge that—

A large hand catches the muffin before its untimely demise. "Watch out," a voice says as the muffin is deposited back on my plate. I turn around, because the voice sounds a lot like Jesse's and . . . Yup, he's standing there. Right beside me. Taking my plate from my hands and setting it on the nearest table, where Kai and Shannon are fighting over the Ubisoft formula.

"Here okay?" he asks, like the kind, attentive gesture he just performed for me is a totally normal occurrence between us.

I nod. Meet his eyes. "Um . . . Thank you?"

"You're welcome."

I want to say more, but one of Nephilim's developers is already hogging Jesse's attention, asking a question about the patches they've been issuing for their most recent game. Jesse nods, a cup of coffee in one hand, a green apple in the other, and I'm forgotten.

I gingerly take a seat and start eating my breakfast.

The muffin turns out to be delicious.

Afterward, Mike and Otto decide that we should go outside and take a group picture, presumably with the purpose of convincing StarPlay that the team-building retreat they are paying handsomely for is, indeed, building a team. I'm not sure how the snowball fight begins—maybe it's John, tripping over Shannon as she makes a snow angel, though it might have been Ashley throwing a ball at Clara and accidentally hitting John. All I know is that it becomes a Nephilim versus FlyButter conflict really fast, and I spend the following twenty minutes shoveling to help Mila build a snow fort.

At which point, I must resentfully admit that while the cotton mittens Aunt Selene crocheted for me are colorful and very cute, they might not have been the best gear for this specific activity. I go through a couple of different stages of misery—freezing pain, wishing for a swift death, wanting to chop off both my hands—but by the time the fort is finally ready I'm mostly feeling numb.

"My fingers are not even cold anymore," I marvel. "I think I've conquered the concept of physical suffering?"

"You haven't," Mila says. "It's just the first step toward hypothermia. Go run your hands under hot water." She runs after Otto, leaving me alone with gruesome visions of frostbite and amputation, and I decide that she's right. I *should* go back inside for a minute.

It's on the porch that I cross paths with Jesse. Again.

He's leaning against one of the wooden columns, eyes never leaving me, and when I'm close enough he says, "You should take your mittens off. They're drenched."

So weird, all these interactions he's been initiating—especially after our disastrous conversation last night. So, *so* weird.

"Yeah." I stand in front of him to shake the snow off the tips of my boots. "I don't think I'm well equipped for this trip. I thought there would be . . . I don't know. Fewer outings, and more sugar cookies."

"I can tell," he says, but there's no bite to it. The opposite, in fact. Because Jesse takes the soaked mittens off my hands, tosses them on the rocking chair right beside us, and wraps his palms around my icy fingers.

My heart, and about half of my internal organs, cease to function.

His grip is warm. Toasty. Delicious, after the stabbing ice of the snow. He smells good. His body shields me from the frigid air, and yet I'm trembling anyway.

"You don't like the snow much, do you?" he asks, like this is a totally normal exchange between us. His tone is . . . well, no different from the way he's been speaking to me for years. Polite but reserved. Except, I pick up on an undercurrent of something else. Something *new*.

"Nope," I say, harnessing my stuttering brain to find my voice. "I hate the cold. You don't?"

"Don't really feel it too much."

I bet. I look up at him, taking in the way he's made, the height and the width, the pink flush on his cheekbones under the rim of his glasses. Suddenly, I don't feel the cold too much, either.

"Do you remember our first meeting?" he asks.

I blink at the abrupt change in topic. "The interview, right? Unless there was another time before . . . ?"

He shakes his head. "Your interview for that programming position. About six years ago." A beat. "Do you remember what happened?"

"I do, actually. The guy made a shitty joke, I got mad, told him he could fuck right off, and stormed out. Then you ran after me and apologized on his behalf." I shrug. "Did I miss anything?"

"Do you remember what you said to me?"

"Yes. Well, not word by word. I had a migraine that day, so it's a bit fuzzy. But I do remember ranting about that guy and this whole industry. Isn't that how it went?"

"Not quite." He exhales. The air around his handsome face blows white. His hands are still wrapped around mine. "Do you remember that I asked you out?"

"You *what?*" I laugh, genuinely amused. "No. No, you didn't. You must be confusing me with . . ." I trail off when I notice the way he's looking at me, like I'm missing a very important puzzle piece, right *there*, at the center of the picture.

I try to recall our conversation. It's all very hazy, but I can almost see Jesse's face in my head, a few years younger, face rounder and more boyish.

Hopeful.

"I was wondering," he said, gently, a little tentative. So different from the firm way he'd spoken to his dickhead of a boss. *"If you . . ."*

I covered my mouth with a yawn. *"Sorry! I'm so tired today—can't believe I stayed up so late to prep to impress that asshole."*

"Don't worry about that. Would you like to get coffee?"

"Oh, no. No, don't worry. Not going to fall asleep at the wheel." I flashed him a grin. *"'Cause I can't afford a car, yet."*

"Ah."

"Oh my god," I say now. "Was it—when you mentioned coffee . . . ?"

He nods. "It occurred to me yesterday, when you told me that I should have just asked you out, that maybe you didn't understand. Because I did ask. And you said no."

I want to crumple into myself and die. "I had no idea! I . . ." He needs to let go of my hands, so I can use them to hide my face and maybe stab myself repeatedly with a pine cone.

But wait. So I didn't catch that he asked me out. I was dumb, okay, but it still doesn't warrant the way he pretended I didn't exist for—

"And then something *else* occurred to me," he continues

gently. "That if you couldn't recall *me* asking you out, maybe you couldn't recall what *you* told me afterward. Do you?"

I shake my head, even as I say, "The rant?"

"The rant was justified. You were upset for very valid reasons. You told me about the challenges of being a woman in such a male-dominated field. Gave me some examples of truly egregious things that happened to you. And one of them was this guy you'd done an internship with, back in college. He asked you out several times, and each time you rejected him. He was insistent, and now that you were both starting to work as developers, you constantly saw him at conferences and workshops. Whenever he was around you felt uncomfortable, and—"

"Oh my god." This time I do free my hands, which tingle pleasantly long past the end of his touch. I take a step back. "You thought I was warning you. You thought that you'd asked me out, I'd rejected you, and then I told you the story to—you thought it was an indirect way to ask you to keep your distance."

He presses his lips together and nods, and . . . He clearly has had a few hours to get used to this screwball piece of misunderstanding, because he appears to see the humor in it. But all I can think of is that shortly after our first encounter, I was going to develop a *massive*, years-enduring, ostensibly unrequited crush on him.

And he'd asked me out.

And I . . .

"I hadn't realized it."

"I know." He thrusts his hands in his pockets. "It became obvious yesterday, when you confronted me."

"So you just . . . You avoided me because . . ."

"I thought it was what you wanted."

"But what about . . . I tried to make conversation with you, several times, and I would smile at you and try to be nice, and—"

"Always in group settings," he points out quietly, biting the inside of his cheek. "I figured that because we had acquaintances in common, you couldn't avoid me. And . . . Viola, you're a nice person. You're nice to everyone. I didn't take you being nice to me as an invitation, and I definitely didn't think it would overwrite the request you'd made of me years earlier—"

"But I didn't! I never made that request, and . . . What about the mistletoe? That was so *mean*!"

He looks away, huffing out an unamused, misty-white laugh. "That one . . . I couldn't stop thinking about how cornered you must have felt, after. But in the moment, it was such a mindfuck, Viola. Because I'd been wanting that kiss for the longest time, and the opportunity was there, served to me like a fucking holiday present. But I also knew how little you wanted me around, and . . ." He shakes his head. His smile is small and wistful, like he finds the fact that we're finally clearing up this years-long misunderstanding funny, but also heartbreaking.

And I think I might be. Heartbroken, that is. Because now that I know that then-Jesse liked then-Viola, I cannot stop remembering how much then-Viola liked him.

"You told my cousin that you wanted nothing to do with me," I say dully.

"You mentioned that, and . . . I don't remember exactly what I said, honestly. But I do recall him asking me why I didn't kiss you, and . . . taking the blame, making it sound like *I* was the one who had issues with you, it seemed fair."

"Fair?"

"Instead of explaining what had happened between us years earlier and—"

"Jesse!" Clara screams from the thick of the snowball fight. "A little help here? We're losing and need someone with powerful arms!"

He sighs indulgently. "Coming!" he yells back, and then, lower, to me: "Here."

I glance at his hand. He's holding out a pair of black, well-insulated snow gloves. They are worn, and made for bigger hands, and . . .

"Oh, no. I can't steal your—"

"Yeah, you can." He takes my wrist and puts the gloves in the palm of my hand. I let him, suddenly, uncharacteristically passive. I think I'm still in a stupor.

"Jesse!" Clara, again. "We're being *decimated.*"

"Yup, coming."

I stare at his back as he jogs to one of the forts, wondering if I hallucinated what he told me. Maybe I was hit in the head by a stray snowball. Maybe I'm lying belly-up on the ground. Maybe life is just a computer simulation.

Jesse's gloves, though, are in my hand, holding a warmth that could come only from his body.

Chapter 11

I GO TO BED AT ELEVEN, BUT GET UP AT ELEVEN THIRTY, WHEN it becomes obvious that all the blankets in the Western Hemisphere are not going to warm me up.

I don't know what my problem is. The thermostat is working fine, which means that the temperature in the room should be perfectly pleasant. And yet, my bones seem to have turned into ice, cooling me from the inside out until I can't lie between the sheets without shivering. Maybe I'm losing my mind. Maybe it's an omen of imminent death. Either way, I'm considering locking myself in the bathroom and running the blow-dryer, just to let my half-frozen brain cells thaw, when I remember the existence of the hot tubs.

There are two. The one closest to my room is, I immediately realize, an absolute no-go: Shannon and Ethan are in it, *alone*, sitting inappropriately close and whispering giggled nothings in each other's ears. Joining them for what is clearly foreplay would traumatize me for life, and my therapy bill is already high enough.

Pass.

I pad my way to the other tub, teeth chattering as the cold air drifts in the folds of my bathrobe. I find that one occupied, too. Otto, Mike, and Jesse are sitting in it, steam wafting between them as they talk about something that looks serious and maybe work-related.

What a choice I am confronted with. I could either chance Shannon and Ethan doing it in front of my very eyes, or spend an as-yet-undetermined amount of time witnessing Mike moon over Otto, Otto tolerate being mooned over, and Jesse . . .

I don't know. I have no idea what Jesse *does*. Things are too complicated with him at the moment, and I'm still reeling with what he told me earlier today, so I decide to silently tiptoe away from the deck.

But.

"Hey, Viola." Mike waves at me with a smile. "You came to soak with us!"

Fuck. "Um, hey. Actually, I was just going to—"

"You can sit over here." He scoots over, making room on

his right. It has the clear advantage of putting him very close to Otto's thigh, while ensuring that I'll be sitting . . . right next to Jesse, of course.

Shit.

"Right. Thank you, Mike."

The water is heaven—if heaven were a delightfully warm pool shared with somewhat questionable company. Although maybe I'm judging the guys too harshly? Mike seems happy to have me around, and even Otto waves at me like he could conceivably imagine enjoying my presence, which makes up for the perennial grimace on his face.

Jesse noticeably averts his gaze the moment I start taking off my bathrobe, and doesn't look back at me until I'm in the water up to my collarbone. Then it's short, furtive glances that don't quite seem to know where to land, as though he's afraid I'm not wearing a swimsuit or something.

Bet you'd hate that, huh? is my first, automatic, confrontational thought. The one informed by the anger and hurt I've cradled since the mistletoe incident. But it falls apart the second I recall recent revelations.

Actually, maybe you wouldn't *hate that. Maybe you wouldn't mind? Maybe you'd even . . .*

That's it. I need to stop. I'm overthinking this for no reason. Jesse simply can't see very well, since his glasses are off again. And he's too busy arguing with Otto over who knows what.

"It's actually way better than *4*—"

Jesse snorts. "Please."

"The map is more postapocalyptic, and the leveling is more interesting than the perk system"—another snort, but Otto ignores him and continues—"*and* the crafting is far superior."

"Doesn't matter, since the story is so weak."

"It doesn't need a strong story, because—"

"Wait," I interrupt. "Are you guys talking about *Fallout 76*?"

They both turn to me. "Yes," Otto says, sounding exceedingly British *and* bored. "Jesse wouldn't know a good game if it bit him in the arse."

I laugh in his face. "Are you kidding me? *Fallout*'s a nightmare. It has no story, no NPCs, no VATS."

"Buggy as hell," Jesse adds, looking mildly nauseous.

"Oh, god, yes. Why did they rush it out? It's unfixable at this point."

"Multiplayer is not that good, either."

"Right—everyone's so spread out. I've been shot, maybe once?"

"For real. And it's dull, no dialogue interactions to manipulate—"

"—right, you're just wandering around, with no consequences to your actions."

"I don't understand why so many people love it."

"Me neither! It's the most overrated—"

Otto rises abruptly to his feet, splashing all of us with hot water. "I'm going to bed," he says crisply, looking between us with narrowed eyes. "And you two are *idiots*."

He gets out of the tub with an unexpected amount of grace. I blink at the sudden reveal of his rosy, freckled skin, and am wondering whether I should apologize when Mike, too, stands.

Unlike Otto, he keeps the splashing to a minimum. "Um—I'm gonna go, too. It's getting late and all that, so . . ."

He vanishes, all but running after Otto, before we can wish him a good night.

I turn to meet Jesse's eyes. "What—what just happened?"

"An impressive display of emotional maturity?" He shrugs, and it's impossible not to notice how broad his shoulders are. The shift of his muscles under the wet skin of his chest.

"Is Otto mad? Did I just single-handedly undo the truce between Nephilim and FlyButter by telling the objective truth about *Fallout*?"

"Nah, don't worry about it. His grudges aren't very long-lasting. And he's probably been masterminding this for a while."

"Masterminding what?"

"An excuse to get some time alone with Mike. Without letting Mike know that he was initiating it, of course."

"You think so?"

"I definitely wouldn't put it past him."

"So—do you think he's still into Mike?"

Jesse tilts his head. "What do you mean?"

"Well, over the years they've been on and off about forty times, and whenever they're broken up Mike is *a mess*, but Otto is always . . . he never seems upset. I kind of assumed that all of Mike's pining was one-sided."

"Are you kidding?" He snorts. "Otto's obsessed. He's very good at hiding any kind of emotion that isn't anger or scorn, but you should see him when he's drunk. He talks about Mike like it's an Olympic sport. He once made me read the poetry he wrote about Mike's *calves*."

"Was it good?"

Jesse winces. Visibly.

"Yeah. I don't even know why I asked."

"You know Mike's family is from Guatemala, right?"

I nod.

"Otto is trying to learn Spanish to make a good impression on them."

"No way!"

"He's being tutored by a multilingual sixteen-year-old who insists on calling him Ocho and forces him to sing the number song every session."

"Oh my god." I laugh into my palm. Should I tell Mike

about this? It's absurd, all this unacknowledged mutual pining. "Why don't they just . . . stay together, if they like each other so much?"

"I'm not sure they are aware of where the other stands."

"Why don't they communicate, then?"

"I don't think it's that simple, Viola." His smile is small, and something about it hits too close to home, reminding me of the conversations he and I had yesterday and . . . was it really just this morning?

Uneasiness sweeps over me, carried by the sudden awareness that with Otto and Mike gone, there are fifty percent fewer people in this hot tub. The air is thick with steam and discomfort, and Jesse and I no longer need to be this close. I should scoot over and sit across from him. But I'm afraid that it might seem like a rejection of sorts, and . . . that's not what I want.

Ask him, urges the voice that dwells inside my head. *Ask him if something changed in the past year. Ask him if he still likes you. Tell him that before he humiliated you in front of your loud, inappropriate family, you used to have a crush on him. Tell him about the sex dreams—*

What? No.

I mentally club the voice with an imaginary baseball bat, forcing it to shut up. I'm *not* subjecting poor Jesse to a non-consensual recap of my horny subconscious. Instead, I swallow, bite the inside of my cheek, and search for something to fill the silence. "So. Tell me what your favorite games are at the moment."

Jesse smiles. His gaze wanders away, to the dark forest and the white tops of the tall pine trees, and I immediately miss it. "This feels like a trick question."

"Yeah, a bit. I can go first, if you want," I offer.

"Please, do." His eyes are back on me. Suddenly, I can't remember what being cold feels like.

"I'm going to start with *Red Dead Redemption 2*, of course—I know you've played that one. With *and* without the corollary drinking game, I assume."

He frowns. "You know—I hate that stupid drinking game so much, and so does Otto. But every time we play it, Ashley is the last one standing by a fucking mile, and every time we tell ourselves that we need a rematch."

I bite back a laugh. Should I reveal Ashley's secret? Nah. Some things Jesse will need to find out for himself. "I believe in you. Never give up on your dreams." I lift my hand out of the tub, meaning to pat his shoulder, but realize at the last minute that touching him *here* and *now* might not be a good idea. My hand hovers awkwardly an inch from his glistening skin before dropping back underwater—and Jesse looks at my movements *the whole time*.

I clear my throat. "Hmm, my second-favorite game is probably *Bloodborne*."

"Good one. It was my reason to live for a couple years."

"Same here. And then . . ." I bite my lower lip. "How weird would it be if I said *Zephyr's Blade*?" It's Jesse's most recent game. And it's so *good*; when it first came out I wanted to punch my own eyes from jealousy—and to cry joyful tears because it existed.

"I don't know." Jesse looks at me, amused. "*Are* you going to say *Zephyr's Blade*?"

I pretend to think about it. "I guess I could. The problem is, I heard that game won a quadrillion awards, and I'm not sure it needs more attention."

"Maybe it *wants* more attention. Specifically, *your* attention."

"Does it?"

Jesse nods. A bit eagerly.

"Well, it's a young game. Still growing. Wouldn't want all the spoiling to mess it up. Therefore, as my third choice, I'll pick *Persona*—"

He makes a face and huffs.

"What?" I ask, defensive. "*Persona*'s good!"

"It has a high school setting," he says flatly.

"Right. Which makes it excellent."

"It makes it dumb."

I gasp.

"Viola, the whole storyline feels like a soap opera, and the world-building is just dull."

"Oh my god, you're so *wrong*." I stand up—and immediately begin shivering in the cold, but power through. "I am going to bed," I proclaim haughtily in a pseudo-British accent, attempting my best Otto impression. "And you"—I point at Jesse—"are an idiot."

He chuckles, shaking his head. "Get back in." His hand comes up to my wrist and tugs me down. "You're one giant goose bump."

I'm not certain what happens after that. Maybe it's Jesse's pull, or the heat fuzzing up my head, or the slippery floor of the tub. I lose my balance—which is a totally normal thing. It has happened to me a million times. Absolutely nothing weird about that.

Nothing, except for the spot where I land.

It's not quite an embrace, but I'm draped awkwardly over Jesse, one arm around his neck while the other holds on to his shoulder for balance. Any other time I'd think that my right breast pushing against his naked chest through my bikini top is very unfortunate, but today I have a more pressing problem.

An *unmistakably* pressing problem, right where my ass meets Jesse's lap.

"I'm sorry," I tell him, scrambling to push away. But that only makes the flesh of my ass drag against his front, and what's happening down there is . . . unequivocal. Unmissable. And Jesse must know that, because it's big.

Huge.

"I . . ." I can think of absolutely nothing to say. I settle for repeating, "I . . ."

Jesse's eyes close, and stay closed as his cheeks color, as he takes a deep breath, as he tells me, "I'm sorry. I didn't mean to . . ." His hand moves up to support my lower back in a gesture that doesn't seem fully voluntary. I think he's making an effort to remain completely immobile, but I feel him vibrating tightly with some sort of tension that . . .

My heart explodes in a gallop. My stomach floods with heat. We are barely touching, and I can't remember the last time I was this turned on.

"So." My voice is a breathy, shaky attempt at humor. "You *do* like me."

His eyes close. "Viola. You have no fucking idea what I feel for you."

This *has* to be one of those dreams I've been having. It's the only possible explanation for the way I decide to respond by wiggling my ass in his lap. But when he feels me move, his lips part to let out a gasp, and his grip hurts for a second.

"Still?" I ask, unable to help myself.

He finally opens his eyes. "Mm?" He is not breathing normally, like people usually do when they're sitting still. And neither am I.

"Well, I know you used to be into me when we first met,

and maybe . . . maybe last year, for the mistletoe. But I wasn't sure if you still . . ."

"Yes. Still." He leans forward. His mouth comes to rest on my collarbone. Not a kiss, but his lips move softly as he speaks against my skin. "I doubt I'll ever stop. Viola, you might want to . . . move away."

"Why?"

"Because I don't . . ."

I think he *does*. He does *a lot*, and this is the hottest thing that has ever happened to me. Bar none. "It's okay." I settle more comfortably on him, feeling his cock twitch. His expression, the way his eyes widen and then almost roll back in his head, it's out of this world. "I don't mind."

His hand tightens involuntarily on my lower back. "You don't?"

"No." No one has ever looked at me this way. Like I could make or break them. Like they don't think they deserve me, but *oh*, they want me. "No, I really don't, and—"

The glass door opens, and the noise is so loud, it startles both of us. I'm not sure who breaks apart first, but the result is the same: One second there is no space between Jesse and me, and the next I'm staring at him from across the tub. We turn at the same time, finding Mike waving at us from the deck entrance.

"I forgot my room key," he says, slightly dejected.

My heart pounds against my ribs. I need Mike to leave. I need to know what happens next between Jesse and me. I need it *right now*.

"Are you guys going to bed, too?" Mike asks.

No, I scream inside my head. There's still heat pulsating sweetly at the base of my stomach, coiling tight inside me. *No, we're staying here. We're finishing this.*

But Jesse says, "We were about to," and lifts himself out of the tub.

I stare at the way the water trickles down his chest and thighs, and it definitely doesn't help things. He finds his glasses and slides them on in a gesture that by now is so recognizably Jesse, I . . . Have I ever found someone this attractive? "Here." He holds the bathrobe out to me, never meeting my eyes.

"Thanks."

Look at me, I order him silently. *Just—look at me. We can continue this upstairs. We can talk about it. We can do whatever we want.*

Jesse nods, walking toward the glass door. "I'm gonna stop by the kitchen and get some water first. See you guys tomorrow."

"Good night," Mike tells him, strolling closer to me, waiting for Jesse to be out of earshot before adding, "Hey, sorry for leaving you guys alone. It didn't occur to me until now that you were stuck with some dude you barely know, alone, in the middle of the night. It was such a dick move."

"No. No, it's fine." I take a deep breath. Massage my temple. Force myself to get out of the tub. "I trust Jesse."

"Okay. Good. I thought so, he's always been a great guy, but I mean . . . They all are until they aren't. You never know when people will turn creepy. You weren't uncomfortable, were you?"

I shake my head, closing the lapels of my robe as the cold seeps once more inside my bones.

Chapter 12

THE FIRST THING I TELL JESSE, RIGHT AFTER HE OPENS THE door and I slip inside his room, yet again uninvited, is: "Thank you for the gloves."

It is, perhaps, an odd thing to say to someone in lieu of hello—especially at three a.m., and especially after knocking on their door at an increasingly loud volume for several minutes, with the obvious intent to wake them up. But I couldn't help myself. After the hot tub I did try to shove what happened out of my mind and to sleep the restlessness away. It was a valiant attempt, one that lasted three whole overwrought hours before I muttered, "Fuck it," and decided to bring all the nervous energy I couldn't get rid of to Jesse's room.

Returning the gloves was the only excuse I was able to think of, and yes, I do feel bad about barging in. Not too bad, though, because it's immediately evident that Jesse wasn't sleeping. Sure, he is wearing green plaid pajama pants that for some Christmas family photo jest of fate happen to exactly match the ones I have on, with a faded black *Minecraft* T-shirt that's clearly an old favorite. But the light of the bedside lamp glows softly, and a book is open facedown on the comforter.

I know exactly what it is, even without reading the title.

"Viola?" He blinks twice. Once more. His glasses are folded on the desk, in front of the TV. "Are you okay?"

"Here," I say, holding out the gloves until he has no choice but to accept them. "I wanted to return them."

"I . . . you can keep them."

"Nah."

"You should. At least until we go back."

"It's okay. I'd probably lose one. Or both. And I have no plans to frolic in the snow ever again." I push the door closed behind me and pad to the bed, taking a seat next to one of the posts with my hands wedged under my thighs. "But it was nice of you to lend them to me. So, thank you."

Jesse shakes his head as if trying to clear it. His hair, those glorious black curls, look a bit wilder than usual. Like maybe he's been running his fingers through them. "You're welcome." He scratches his jaw, and I begin to suspect that he has no clue what to do with his hands. "What are you doing here, Viola?"

What a good question. An excellent question. I pondered it as I tried to talk myself out of coming here, but I still got out of bed, slid a long-sleeved T-shirt over my tank top, and knocked on Jesse's door. Go figure.

"Nothing. I just thought maybe we could . . ."

We could continue, I mean to say. *With what we were doing in the hot tub a few hours ago. Because I haven't been able to stop thinking about it, and I'm going crazy, just from the knowledge that you're in the next room over. That you exist.*

But all I can bring myself to tell Jesse is, "We could talk."

". . . Talk?"

I nod. "Talk."

"About what?" He looks wary, and also far away. Like he's trying to keep his distance in more ways than one.

"I don't know. We could talk about a lot of things. We could bash *Fallout 76* a little more, or you could recite a curated selection of the poetry Otto wrote for Mike, or you could tell me if that copy of *The Sunken Heart* is yours. I initially thought it must be from the library here, but after yesterday's meeting I'm not so sure. We could chat about that weird triathlon stuff you and Ashley love so much, or . . . I don't know. The weather is always a favorite." My hand comes up to fidget with the tips of my hair. It's gotten too long, and I should get it cut, but leaving it down was a good idea. Gives me something to do. "Or we could talk about what happened earlier today."

Jesse swallows and runs his palm down his face. His answer is a long time coming. "It was technically yesterday," he mutters.

I huff out a laugh. "Right. I mean, it's an incredibly pedantic thing to point out, but nevertheless true."

"Jesus." He pinches the bridge of his nose, looking apologetic and defeated. "I was way out of line."

"No. You weren't."

"I was. It's just that whenever you're around . . . It has been a problem. I've thought about you so much through the years, but I seem to be unable to *not* fuck up when I'm with you." He takes a deep breath. "You were very close. I lost control. Badly. And—"

"I don't mind," I hasten to push in. And when he still looks like he couldn't possibly believe me, I nod forcefully. "For real. I don't. It's kind of . . ." *flattering*, I almost say. But I think it might be construed the wrong way. I'm not here, in this room, because *someone* wants me. I'm here because that someone is *Jesse*. Because he's . . . God, I can't look away from him. From that shallow dimple that seems to appear only when he clenches his jaw. "It's fine."

"Is it?" He doesn't seem convinced, so I rise from the

bed and walk closer to him, until we're standing in front of each other.

And then, at last, I let it out. "I used to have a crush on you," I confess. It turns out to be a wonderfully easy thing to do.

His lips twitch into a small smile. "It's nice of you to say, but—"

"No. Jesse, this is not a let's-spare-the-boy's-feelings situation. I used to have a crush on you. For years. It started the second time we met, and it continued for . . . a long time. It didn't end until last year, with the stupid mistletoe, and only because your actions and what you told my cousin were such an obvious rejection, I couldn't help being angry. I refused to allow myself to like you. But even when I was dating this other guy, I had a crush on you, and also a lot of . . ." I glance around, wondering how to phrase it. Then go with, "Impure thoughts."

His eyes widen. "Impure thoughts."

"Interpret that as you will. The point is, I don't mind that you're into me." I'm barefoot, and he's so tall, so solid, I can feel the heat he emanates even without touching him. "I welcome it, actually."

Jesse looks lost for a moment, frowning like he needs time to decode what I said, the implications of it. After a while his lips part and his mouth moves to form three simple words. "Are you sure?"

"Very," I say, stepping a little closer.

He looks overwhelmed and conflicted, as taut as a bowstring. I suspect that his brain might be about to explode—and then he takes a step back. "The thing is, Viola, it's costing me a lot, and I want to punch myself for saying this, I truly do, but . . . If what you want is to get laid, I'm not the right person for it."

"Really?" I frown. Cock my head. "Earlier it felt like you might be."

He exhales a laugh. "Yes. Really."

"Why?"

"Many reasons, but . . ." He scratches the side of his neck. "Mainly, I don't think I'd be very good at keeping things casual."

"Oh." I step into him, and now we are actually touching. Just barely, mostly our clothes, but it's *almost* enough. "Have you only had sex with people you were in serious relationships with?"

Jesse shakes his head, but doesn't move back, nor does he take his eyes off me. "I've had sex with people I barely knew. That's not it."

"So, what you're saying is . . ." I lift my hand to his shoulder, feeling the lovely warmth of his skin through the thin cotton. "Historically, with other people, you *have* been good at keeping things casual."

Jesse tucks his chin into his chest and says, "Historically. Yes."

I nod. "So what's the problem? If you've done it before, then you could—"

"The problem is that other women were not you." His eyes stay locked with mine, and something hot and full explodes in my chest. Without realizing it, I've moved my hand to his face; I cup his cheek, soft and freshly shaven, and watch as his throat bobs. "With you, I have to be careful. Because I don't just *like* you, Viola. I didn't meet you at a bar and think that you were pretty. I didn't have fun on a blind date and decide to take you home. I have thought of you every day for years. I've pictured you in ways that, believe me, you do not want to hear. I have a whole mental list of stuff to go through with you, and if we start something, it's not going to just *end* for me. It's going to stick, and it *is* going to grow out of proportion, and it's going to have the capacity to rip me apart. Especially since you and I are going to be working very closely together for the next couple of years." His lips curve into a small, sad smile. "I know it's early. I know you don't know me well. I'm not saying that I refuse to be with you until you promise that you'll marry me. Lots of relationships start with the best intentions and still don't work out. But if you're here because you're thinking that some no-strings-attached sex would be fun . . ." He wraps his fingers around my wrist, the one hovering by his cheek, but doesn't push me away. He holds me there as time stretches between us, sweet and uncertain. "That's not where I'm at, Viola."

What he just said, I cannot yet comprehend it. And at the same time, I understand it perfectly. It's the reason my heart beats into my chest, my stomach, my temples. The reason my mouth is dry and my throat full. "I have a proposal."

He nods and waits for me to continue.

"What if you and I were to . . . hang out, together, for the next couple days. And do whatever it is that we want—from, I don't know, making out, to playing video games, to getting to know each other better. Anything goes. And by the time we get back to Seattle, we could reassess the situation and see whether . . ." I smile. Bite into my lip. "We could see whether there is something here. Something to be had."

Jesse says nothing and studies me with clear, limpid eyes. I force myself to be patient, tell myself that I'll take whatever answer he gives—when the corner of his mouth twitches upward.

He leans in and nuzzles his cheek into my hand. "Something to be had," he murmurs, his words laced with humor and a warmth that sounds a lot like eagerness.

I push up on my toes and smile against his lips.

Chapter 13

OVER THE YEARS I'VE HAD A LOT OF FIRST KISSES, BUT none as perfect as the one I share with Jesse, with his hand in my hair and the tip of my toes on top of his feet. I think he must agree, because once we start, we're not able to stop.

We make out like teenagers. Not that I ever experienced anything like this when I *was* a teenager, but the description fits. We lie on Jesse's bed, stretched out over the comforter, and for hours not a single stitch of clothing comes off. We kiss, and kiss, and kiss, and every time Jesse's hands come anywhere close to slipping underneath my shirt, or into the waist of my pants, he seems to change his mind and slowly retreats, as though he's not ready to move on to the next stage—as though this first one is too good to be left behind so soon.

It's okay. Because I'm not bored. In fact, my mind is being blown right out of my skull. I desperately, helplessly fall in love with the way he groans when his tongue first meets mine, and the bruising grip of his hands on my hips while I lick a soft, salty spot on his throat; that sharp intake of our breaths once he finally gives in and rubs his palm against my breast, my nipples hard and pointy through the thin cloth of my shirt. And then there's the trembling in his fingers as he runs them through my hair, how he arches off the bed after I bite his earlobe, but most of all it's the things he tells me. And the things he clearly wants to say but doesn't quite manage to let out.

"You're so—" as I straddle his waist and lean over him, my hair a thick curtain insulating us from the rest of the world.

"I used to dream of you doing this," when I let my fingers slide up and down the fine hair underneath his belly button.

And: "Viola. If we don't slow down a little, this is going to get very embarrassing very soon—*shit*," just a few seconds after I start rocking on top of him. The friction of his cock against me is the closest I've ever come to a true out-of-body experience. My clit pulses. I hear the raspy pleading in his tone, and let out a breathless laugh.

This is nothing. We have done next to nothing, and it's

already the best sex of my entire life, equally frustrating and delicious in a way that has me soaking through the cotton of my underwear and trying to get closer, closer, get Jesse to live under my skin to fill this new hollow inside me.

"Is this okay?" he asks me whenever he pushes things forward, even just an inch.

"Is this okay?" I ask him a few times, pressing kisses on his full mouth and trying to lean back to look into his eyes. He just forcefully pulls me back to him, and my head is warm and buoyant, filled with sharp pleasure and heat.

We keep going until the night dies out and the dawn breaks. Then Jesse hears the loud rumbling in my stomach, and the touch of his hands abruptly stops. He is bent over me but lifts his head to look at me. His lips are so bee-stung that I cannot help but chase them and swipe across them with my tongue.

He smiles. Nips a little bite on the corner of my jaw. "I'll go downstairs. Bring back some breakfast." His voice is low and husky, and it'll stick with me forever. I *know* I'll hear it on my deathbed.

"No," I protest. "Stay."

"I'll be just a second."

I sigh and close my eyes, already resigned. "I'll come with you, then."

"Stay, please." His mouth, pressed against my neck. "I like knowing that you're waiting for me in my bed."

He clears his throat and pulls back with some difficulty, sitting on the edge of the bed and facing away from me. I stare at his back from the pillow, marveling at how well-built he is. After experiencing firsthand how much I had to spread my legs to sit astride him, I probably shouldn't be this surprised.

But Jesse remains still for a long moment, and as I study him I realize that his muscles are stiff and rigid with a tension I'm not sure I understand.

I sit up right behind him. "Are you okay?"

"Yeah. I—" His deltoid is rock hard under my hand. "I need a second. Probably better if you don't touch me for a little while." He says it calmly, but there is some grit in his voice, and that's when I look down at his lap and realize exactly what's going on.

"Oh. Are you . . ." I'm not sure what to ask. "Can I do anything?"

He shakes his head, clearly amused. "I just need a minute."

I make to pull back to give him space to get himself under control, but it doesn't sit right with me. Leaving him alone, like this. When all I want is to . . .

I hug him from behind and lay my chin on his shoulder. "Maybe a minute is not what you need," I whisper in his ear. My breasts press against his back, and I can feel all his muscles tighten at once.

"Viola."

"Maybe . . ." I kiss him behind the ear, wondering if he can feel my heartbeat. "Maybe, what you *really* need is to get off."

He exhales a sharp, breathy laugh, like the prospect of coming—of me making him come—just punched the air out of his lungs. This could be the most erotic moment of my entire life. A good contender for the top three, for sure.

And that's *before* I ask against his temple, "Would you like that, Jesse?" and he makes that sound—that shapeless, involuntary grunt that makes me clench around nothing.

He is shivering. Or maybe he wasn't, but he definitely starts when my palm traces the tent in his pants, which juts out at an impressive angle. It's already wet with precome, and I can't help but run my teeth up and down the column of his throat as I slide my hand inside the opening of his pajama bottoms.

He is, of course, not wearing anything underneath. How interesting. How convenient. How *perfect*.

"May I?" I ask with a kiss on his cheek, and Jesse doesn't answer or nod, but arches against my hand just enough that the *Please, please continue* doesn't need to be spoken out loud. His eyes track my fist around his cock. His fingers almost rip the sheet from the mattress, and I feel like a sex goddess.

"Fuck," he murmurs, and I wonder how to interpret that. Then realize that I could just ask.

"Does it feel good, Jesse?" I begin to pump, up and down in slow, steady pulls. His cock feels as glorious as it did when pressed against me. I wonder if I should switch to using two hands. I wonder if Jesse is aware of how much I like his body. "Is this how you like it?"

He groans, "Viola." His head falls back, and I let my lips graze the cut of his jaw.

"You can tell me." My hand continues to move, down to his tight balls and then up the shaft again, and it feels as if pleasure is spilling out of all of him—his cock, his vocal cords, his spine. "When you're alone, when you do it to yourself, is this what you do?"

"Fuck, I'm going to—" His hips jerk upward, straining to meet my palm.

"You can tell me," I repeat, twisting my wrist. He grunts and goes rigid, arching even more into me. "How you prefer it. And I'll do it. I just want to make you . . ."

When he comes, he's completely silent. In fact, he stops breathing for a moment, right before pushing through and going off all over my hand and his stomach, and I . . . I try to recall if I've ever enjoyed doing this as much as I am now. I love watching him gasp for air, his hand that suddenly reaches for my leg, as if to anchor himself, his mouth shaping my name, awed and soundless.

I could have my own orgasm just by staring at his. Absorb all the pleasure leaking from him into myself.

"Good?" I ask with a soft smile after a while, when the beat of his heart seems to have steadied under my lips.

Jesse's throat bobs in a small, jerky movement. I make to wipe my palm over my pants, but he surprises me by grabbing my wrist and knitting our fingers together, then bending his head as if to stare at a masterpiece he's woven. It's the sweetest, filthiest of handholds.

My other arm comes up to wrap around his shoulders, and we stay like that for a long time, watching the snow that has once more begun to fall outside.

"Yeah," he says eventually. "Good."

Chapter 14

♥♥♥♥♡

WE EAT IN THE CHAIRS BY THE WINDOW, THE SMALL ROUND table between us, my legs crossed and his stretched out. He watches me dig into the plates he carried upstairs—most of them piled with food for me. For himself, he took only some eggs and a green apple. I smile around a mouth of toast, wondering why he would pick the sourest piece of fruit at the buffet table.

And then I remember that things between us have changed. We're getting to know each other. I can ask him.

"It's an apple," he says with an amused shrug. "All apples taste the same, Viola."

"Wow. You truly have an abundance of terrible opinions.

First *Persona*, now this." He lets out an exaggerated sigh, and I offer him my Danish. "Want some?"

He shakes his head. "I don't have a big appetite in the mornings." It's so *exciting* to discover things about him—his habits, his preferences, his needs. I nod, even though I can't relate at all, and tuck it away for the future.

"I love having a big breakfast."

"I know." He notices my raised eyebrows and continues, "We've been at a bunch of conferences together through the years. I've seen you eat."

I finish chewing, trying not to get lost in the choked, wistful feeling that comes with knowing that he was looking at me the whole time, even as I believed he was indifferent. "In case you're silently judging me for the amount of saturated fatty acids I'm packing in . . . thank you for not saying it out loud."

"Do people do that?"

"My family? All the time. Whenever I'm home, it's a constant commentary on the macronutrients I put into my mouth."

"That's intrusive. And needless?" He sounds like he couldn't possibly care less about what I eat.

"Okay." I chuckle. "I know how you athletic types are, and I'm not exactly a health nut, so—"

"You're perfect." He sounds so serious and earnest, I can't hold his gaze any longer.

I eat a few grapes, and then ask: "Did you and Ashley ever date?"

His eyes widen. "No, never. Where is this coming from?"

"I don't know. In the car ride here you two seemed . . . comfortable with each other. And like you have lots of things in common. Sports and stuff."

"Is that how you pick the people you date? Comfort and shared interests?"

I mull it over. My latest boyfriend loved archery and playing the clarinet—and I had no interest in either. "Not really," I say. "Although my ex and I had nothing in common, and then broke up out of sheer mutual boredom after two years together, so maybe I *should* pay more attention to that stuff?" I take a sip of coffee. "What about you? Who was the last person you dated?" I scrunch my face the second the words are out of my mouth. "I'm sorry. Is it okay to ask? I don't want to be intrusive."

"You can ask me whatever you want, Viola. That's the whole point."

There is something in the way he says it that makes me flush.

"I saw someone for about six months. She was not in the industry—a high school teacher. We broke up . . . exactly a year ago, actually."

"Right before the holidays?"

He nods.

"What happened?"

A small smile. "After the mistletoe incident, it seemed a little unfair. Continuing with her, that is." My heart flutters like a hummingbird. He lets his half-eaten apple dangle from its stem before setting it back on the table. "And then I haven't dated much in the past year, not even casually, because of how busy I was with *Zephyr's Blade*."

"Same here." I smile when something occurs to me. "I was thinking that . . . I've seen a lot of industry couples break up, and I've always hated how weird things can get afterward, both personally and professionally. That's why I avoided any sort of entanglement with colleagues. As you know from my . . . rant."

"I do know."

"But if it's the right person . . . I think that it might be nice. Being with someone who understands the pressure of crunch, and how hectic the weeks leading up to a release can be. Someone who loves games as much as I do. Don't you think?"

With anyone else, I would cut out my own tongue before saying something like this, something full of presumptions hinting that by the time we're on a tight deadline again, we might still be together. With Jesse, though, I feel no embarrassment. I watch the quiet pleasure that blooms on his face at my words, and feel it mirrored by the warmth in my chest.

"I agree," he says, simple, quiet.

I stare at him like a mooning fool until a yawn bubbles up my chest and breaks the spell. "I'm probably going to have to nap at some point today. I don't do very well on no sleep at all."

"Me neither." He picks up his apple again. "You can nap here."

I bite my lower lip, turning to the window to hide another smile. "Is it going to stop, you think? The snow?"

"I met Mike downstairs—he said that it's supposed to go on for a while. The slopes are off-limits. Lots of people went back to bed."

It's as if overnight, a huge, white blanket was laid on top of the lodge and the surrounding woods. The dark green of the pine trees has dulled, wrapped in thick sheets of snow. I try to remember the last time I've felt quiet like this, and come up with nothing. "What if we get snowed in?" I ask Jesse.

He shrugs, and the corner of his mouth curves up.

It wouldn't be all that bad, I think, smiling back at him.

■ ■ ■ ■ ■

ONCE HE HAS ME NAKED AND STANDING BETWEEN HIS OPEN LEGS, Jesse just stares at me. For *forever*.

He's sitting on the edge of the bed, still fully dressed, and taking me in, his gaze dark and intent as it roams over slopes and flatlands. I've always considered myself lucky, because I've never developed any self-consciousness about my body, but the way Jesse's eyes track every inch of my skin would be enough to make even an Instagram model uneasy.

"Want to take a picture?" I ask, hoping a joke will swallow my discomfort. "Actually, do not take a picture. You're *not* allowed. Not that I don't trust you, but I'm not sure what kind of cybersecurity measures you've taken to protect your data, and if your cloud gets hacked I—"

His thumb comes up to press on my lips, and his expression has an odd quality to it, at once profoundly calm and desperate. I realize that what he wants is some time and quiet to process this.

To process *me.*

"Anyway." My lips curve against the fleshy part of his thumb. I bite delicately, playfully into it. "This is me."

Jesse sighs and leans forward, pressing a soft, open-mouthed kiss right below my sternum. "Yesterday, when you walked on the deck and took off your robe . . ." He doesn't continue immediately. Just wraps both hands around my waist until my breath catches. I'm already very wet. "I tried so hard to be good and not to stare. But it's fucking impossible. You make it *impossible.*"

I think he might have a thing for my tits, judging from the way he licks my nipples into his mouth, suckles lightly on the plump sides. He's good at this, as good as he is at designing games and leading a team and who knows how many other things, so I comb my fingers through his hair, lean into him, and try to keep the sounds coming from my throat at a dignified volume, in case someone happens to wander into our part of the lodge.

I don't quite succeed.

"What can I do?" he whispers huskily as I wriggle out of his grip, wanting to peel his shirt off. "What can I do to you?"

I tug at his sleeve. "I need this to *go*."

He obeys, and his body is so beautiful, I don't know where to rest my eyes. The spot where the muscles in his shoulder meet his neck, the curve of his biceps, the way the light hair at the bottom of his abdomen disappears into his jeans. I want those off, too, so I pull him on the bed with me, my fingers flying to his belt as he takes my face into his hand.

"You taste like strawberries," he tells me, sucking my lips, kissing me like he has already memorized each corner of my mouth. "What can I do?" he asks again, and I . . .

"What do you *want* to do?"

Jesse leans back, his Adam's apple visibly moving. "You have no fucking idea, Viola." He looks apologetic. And hopeful. "The things I've been thinking about . . ."

I can't help but smile. I take his hand between mine, bringing his palm to my mouth. "Why don't you show me?"

I think this is what he needed—permission to do exactly *that*. He groans, and moves lower down my body, burying his nose in my belly and inhaling deeply. And then he effortlessly flips us around, until I'm on my knees facing his feet and his face is between my legs, and before I can orient myself or process his intentions, he's already licking up into me.

I gasp.

"Fuck," he grunts. "I hoped you'd be wet."

Honestly, *drenched* would be a more apt descriptor, and I exhale in surprise, slamming my palm on my mouth.

He lets out another deep groan, runs his palms up my thighs to my butt, and as he licks between my folds, he pulls me down to better meet his mouth. I lean back and blindly search for support, trying to find balance on my knees, and end up holding on to one of the posts. I don't know why, but I didn't think that the first thing he'd want to do with me would be having me kneel on his face. And yet, the way his tongue and teeth work against me is simply *unreal*. Like this is a plan he had, something he's been plotting for a while.

"I've been dreaming about this," he says, his nose brushing against my lips and making me shiver. He moans before licking carefully around my opening. "For *years*."

I want to know more. I want every little detail of every single thing he has imagined. I want to know if it's living up to his expectations, but he nips at my inner thigh, and my mind snaps blank for a minute. He's so *good* at this. Talented. A man on a mission, single-minded and dedicated, with just the right amount of pressure and suction, and my nerve endings are about to explode. I feel addled, dizzy with the pleasure of it.

"You taste even better than I expected," he says, hoarse and a little incredulous. When he takes my stiff, swollen clit between his lips, it's like a fist wrapping around my lower belly.

But I don't want to come, not yet. Not when there's more of *this* to have. "Can you—can you give me a minute to . . ." I look down, to the jeans I never managed to take off him. His erection is a long and hard imprint against the fly, and after a moment to balance myself, I lean forward, my palms coming to rest on each side of his hips. Once I'm steady, I take out his cock, the catch of the zipper mixing with the wet sounds rising from his mouth.

"You don't have to—" he mumbles, but I'm fast, and sloppy with pleasure, not thinking it through before lowering myself. Just by having him in my mouth, the pleasure pooling in my stomach tightens and deepens. My thighs clench and release, and I rock against his face as I take him deeper in my throat.

"Shit, Viola. Shit."

We come at the same time, and it feels so good, it shoots me into a whole new world.

■ ■ ■ ■ ■

I SHOWER IN HIS ROOM.

There is no reason for it. My room is less than ten feet

away, with my towels and my shampoo and my body wash and my clean clothes. The phone I haven't checked in over twelve hours—a first in my adult life—is there, too. Using my own bathroom would be the sensible, convenient thing to do, but Jesse takes my hand and asks me not to go.

"Not yet," he says, calm, unglued like I've never seen him, his hand cupping the back of my head, and I don't even need to say yes. I just relax into him and let him lead me to his shower to wash every nook and cranny of my body, lingering and thorough and oddly familiar, as though this were a habit, one time out of many and not the first.

Jesse is hard throughout, but when I offer to do something about it, he shakes his head, and bends down to lick the water from my skin. He laughs quietly when I try to return the favor and wash his hair—I can't quite reach, and he has to pick me up, hands under my ass as I wrap my legs around his waist like he's the sturdiest of tree branches.

We kiss. Endlessly. We kiss until the skin of my fingers becomes pink and wrinkly, and his cock gets even harder, his heartbeat faster. Eventually I take pity on him and bring him off with slow, lazy pulls, licking the protest away from his lips until a shiver runs through his spine and come mixes with soap suds in the shower drain. He towels me off and gently retaliates, his fingers a little fumbling but deliciously thick and eager, his mouth unbearably skilled, and my mind whites out as my body blossoms with a sweet, clinging pleasure that makes me forget myself for long, long moments.

This, I think while attempting to catch my breath, my hand running through Jesse's damp hair as he nibbles idly on my hip bone, *is not at all how I thought this retreat would go.*

Chapter 15

"DO IT LIKE . . . THAT BRAID."

I pause in the middle of pulling up my hair and look at Jesse over my shoulder. He's lying against the headboard, not even pretending to do anything besides stare at me performing the most mundane of tasks. All this attention could be unsettling, maybe should be, but after learning how hard he tried not to look, and for how many years, it makes me feel . . . warm.

"What braid?"

"The one that starts high at the top of your head."

"You mean, a French braid?"

He shrugs. "You had it at PNW GameCon, three years ago. On the second day of the expo."

"Oh my god." I laugh. "There is no way you remember what my hair was like at some random con, let alone on which day."

He simply blinks at me, a hint of a challenge in his eyes.

I turn, hands on my hips. "Okay. What was I wearing?"

"Jeans and a white T-shirt."

He's right. The funny thing is that normally *I* wouldn't remember what I was wearing, but that day FlyButter took a team picture, which currently hangs in our headquarters' entrance. I pass it every time I take the elevator. "Do you have an eidetic memory, or . . . ?"

"Or."

The unsaid is almost explicit: It's only when it comes to *me* that he's been storing up details for years, cataloging every piece of available information, hoarding them like small treasures.

I lean against the dresser. "What other clothes of mine do you like?"

He doesn't have to think it through for very long at all. "You own a dress. Striped."

"Pink and white?"

He nods.

"What do you like about it?"

"It's lovely." He shrugs, like that's all. And then adds with a self-effacing, almost sheepish smile, "It's a little shorter and tighter than what you usually wear, so it made me . . . Things happened, when you wore it." I have no idea how to reply to that, which is just as well, since Jesse continues with: "But I like all your clothes."

I smile and face the mirror again, sectioning damp strands of hair for the braid Jesse asked for. He requested so nicely, after all. And I don't mind playing DJ for him. In fact, the idea makes my heart beat twice as fast.

"Do you think it'll work out?" I ask distractedly. "*Limerence 3.* FlyButter and Nephilim?"

He nods without hesitating. "It will. I'll make sure that it does. I've been wanting to work with you since I first saw your portfolio."

I turn around but keep working on my hair. "It was you, wasn't it? That interview where I met you . . . You were the one who picked my résumé out of the pile, not your boss."

"That guy wouldn't know talent if it ran him over on the highway."

"But you do?"

Jesse shrugs. "It doesn't take a practiced eye to see how brilliant you are."

I am tempted to glance away and minimize what he told me—but he's right. I *am* good at what I do. Instead, I say, "I have another dress."

Jesse doesn't comment on the abrupt change of topic and waits for me to continue.

"It's pale yellow and orange. Longish."

"I don't remember that one."

"You wouldn't. It's a bit too dressy for conferences or work. But I was thinking of wearing it for Chelsea's ceremony." My cousin. Who's marrying his former college roommate. Jesse's in the wedding party—just like I am.

"I look forward to seeing it."

I pick up a hairband and start tying the end of my braid, thinking that in the next few months we're going to be meeting quite a lot. Work. Family functions. The thought felt like a nightmare a couple of days ago, but . . . no longer. Not at all. I walk to the bed, and a moment later he's pulling me into him. "Hey," he murmurs against the skin of my throat.

I smile into his hair. Just a little. "Hey."

■ ■ ■ ■ ■

DURING DINNER, I REACH A MAJOR REALIZATION: JESSE NEEDS TO stop staring at me like *that*, or *everyone* is going to figure out exactly what's going on between us.

I don't habitually care much about what my colleagues think, not when it comes to my personal life, but considering that *Limerence 3* is at stake, a romantic relationship between lead designers feels like something better kept close to the vest. Would the publisher consider it a liability? Would they fear a messy breakup and subsequent delays in development? Would they strip the lead designer title from either of us? I have no idea. The thought does worry me a little, but it's hard to work up a lot of anxiety, especially after spending the perfect day with Jesse.

I can't get over the simplicity of it. We spent a few hours fooling around and talking about video games, the places we've been and the ones we want to travel to, how lonely it was for him to grow up as an only child and how irritating for me to have a million siblings.

"It sounds fun," he said, thumb sweeping over my cheekbone. "Always having people around."

"That's the problem: There was *always* someone around, making noise. I didn't fully comprehend the concept of silence until I was in college. You remember the way my family sounded at the engagement party?"

"How could I forget."

"That was all day. Every day. For *eighteen* years."

He smiled. "Sometimes chaos is better than silence."

"Yeah?" I snuggled closer. "What were your parents like?"

"Gone, for the most part. I was on my own a lot. But there were pros, too."

"How so?"

"Let's just say that I got to play lots of age-inappropriate games from a young age."

"Please, tell me you weren't playing *Grand Theft Auto* at seven or anything like that."

"Oh, Viola." A brief kiss. "You know I can't do that."

We took a nap, Jesse curled around me, which warmed me up fully for the first time since coming here. When we woke up, the first thing I saw was his sleepy, happy smile, as though he couldn't imagine anything better than finding me next to him, and I couldn't help tracing its contours.

It just . . . fills me with immense joy. Being with him. Telling him things. Waiting to hear what he'll say back. Being reminded of his existence.

Still, he should focus on his salad, or on the conversation that Ashley and Kai have been trying to rope him into—anything but me, because whenever I feel his eyes on any part of my body, I can't help but stare back.

"We might get stuck here," Mike is saying at our table, squirting ketchup on his fries. "If it doesn't stop snowing. Not sure what's going to happen weather-wise, the forecasts have been kind of hit or miss."

We are scheduled to leave the lodge tomorrow night. Normally, I'd loathe the prospect of being kept from the cozy quiet of my apartment for a few more hours, but not this time.

I risk a glance at Jesse. Who is, of course, still staring at me.

Oh, well. We exchange a small, private smile, and it's not the end of the world. No one notices, and no one cares, even as my heart nearly explodes.

"What time are we supposed to leave?" Shannon pours some more wine into her glass.

"Around five or six p.m. If the roads are accessible," Mike says. "We're kind of snowed in as of right now, but the plows will be running soon."

Shannon clasps her hands together. "So what you're saying is, tonight may *not* be our last night here. But it also *may* be."

"Correct."

"We need to figure out something extra fun, then."

I scratch the tip of my nose, and the smell of Jesse is suddenly here, all around me. It's delicious. After we get back to town, I'll go to the grocery store and stock up on his brand of body wash.

"Oooh." Mila leans forward. "How about we do another movie marathon?"

"Veto on anything *Transformers*," Kai says.

"Oh, man." Ethan leans back against his chair, pouting like a five-year-old.

"It's for the best." Shannon pats his back. "I think I saw the *Indiana Jones* DVDs."

"Good one."

"I haven't seen *Temple of Doom* in years."

"Okay, but we're not watching *Crystal Skull*, right?"

"God, no."

"Still better than *Transformers*."

"Oh, shut up."

"Listen—not all *Transformers* movies are created equal—"

"Viola," Mila interrupts, stealing a fry from Mike's plate. "You okay with *Indiana Jones*?"

"Oh." I smile, sliding my chair back a few inches and rising to my feet. "I'm tired, actually. I think I'll go to bed early today."

Ethan frowns up at me. "You've been in bed all day. Are you sick?"

"Nope. Just a small headache."

"I thought those bad migraines stopped when you started those meds?"

"They did." I pick up my empty plate and fork. "I don't think that's what I have. I just need to catch up on sleep."

"How many hours can one possibly sleep in a day?"

I bite the inside of my cheek. "I'll count and report back?"

"I get it, though," one of Nephilim's programmers says through a mouthful of focaccia. "The mattresses here are so fucking comfortable."

"What—no! They're way too soft. It's scoliosis waiting to happen . . ."

I sneak away from the table as the lumbar-health argument heats up, quickly disposing of my dirty plate and grabbing a bottle of mango juice to take upstairs. Behind me, I notice Otto stands by Jesse's chair, leaning forward to talk to him.

"I'm willing to forget what you said about *Fallout* and play *Red Dead Redemption* with you," I overhear him say. His upper lip is not as curled as usual. "Even though you are wrong. And an idiot."

When I turn around and head for my room, my eyes meet Jesse's. There is a glint in them—one I've recently come to recognize.

"That's very magnanimous of you," I hear him reply right before stepping out. "But no, thanks."

Chapter 16

EARLIER TODAY, IN A HUSHED CONVERSATION, WE TOLD EACH other that it would be best not to have sex, not until we got back to Seattle and got our hands on some condoms. In the end, though, we cannot resist.

I have an IUD. Neither of us has ever had unprotected sex before. Maybe it's a little foolish, maybe we're irresponsible.

Fine—we *are* irresponsible.

Nevertheless, it's a conscious choice that we make. Jesse licks me until I'm pink and raw, stretches me open with his fingers, and even waits for long moments before sliding inside, rocking against my folds while holding himself on top of me with trembling arms. He seems to hesitate, like he's afraid to hurt me, like he thinks that if he lets himself do this I'll disappear.

I find it maddening, his restraint. Adorable, too. So I whisper, "Let me get you started," right in his ear, and wrap my legs around his hips to force him to sink deep.

"It's okay," I say, a little out of breath, because I can tell that he's about to ask. He looks worried and feverish and a little wild, so I press a kiss into the chiseled line of his jaw, then another, and repeat, "I'm okay."

"Good," he says, though it sounds airy, like he's mostly exhaling. "Good." And then he attempts a thrust—just pulls back less than an inch, pushing in to the hilt again, and—maybe I'm *not* okay after all.

"Wait. Wait." I arch, trying to make more room inside, afraid I'll burst at the seams. I've never been this . . . I don't even know how I feel.

"Want me to pull out?" His voice is strained. I appreciate the offer, especially because of how costly and earnest it sounds.

"Is that an option?" I ask with a smile.

He frowns. "Of course. If you ask me to stop, I'll always—"

"Here." I push at his shoulder, sweat-slick and rock-hard. "Let me be on top."

It helps. I can adjust the depth and angle of him, and the

burn is suddenly nice. Jesse likes it, too: He pushes my legs apart to stare at my shiny folds, open around him. His fingers tighten around my thighs, and he groans a noise that's low and animallike. I lean forward to kiss him sweetly on the mouth, and he quiets down, his muscles losing some of that trembling tension.

"Is this okay?" I ask. "This position?"

He nods without opening his eyes. His hands slide up to my waist, my rib cage, and then move down to grip the flesh of my ass. He might be leaving bruises. I hope he is. "I don't know how long I can . . ." His jaw clenches. "Next time I'll probably last longer. Maybe. But this first . . ."

"Don't worry about it." He is so deep, I can almost taste him in my mouth. But I'm getting used to him. "You can come, if you need to."

Jesse squeezes his eyes shut. The muscles in his stomach ripple, tight and restless. "If I *need*—oh, fuck."

He probably wasn't ready for me to start moving, but I can't help myself. I roll my hips, looking for a good rhythm, for the pressure against that place deep inside me. The burning stretch of him aches so deliciously, I cannot contemplate stopping. I lower myself to him, and can feel his heart, a beating flutter against mine, as the heat begins to tingle in my abdomen and push up, then down, then up again. "This way, Jesse? You like it like this?"

He doesn't reply, but his yes reverberates throughout my

body nevertheless. Because his hands swallow my hips, and then *he*'s the one taking charge and moving me around his cock, and it's so *good*, I forget how to breathe. He grunts, bites my shoulder, and when his control is on the verge of snapping in two, he slides his hand between our bodies and begins circling my clit with his thumb, making my orgasm rise and swell in powerful waves.

"Viola." He breathes against my mouth, and all I'm aware of is his touch, his scent, his voice, the heat spilling in my belly. "You are the best thing in this entire fucking world."

I don't hear the rest, because my body begins to contract around him, and I'm coming in a wash of burning pleasure. I sag on top of his chest, trying to stifle my whimpers into the skin of his sternum, and that's when Jesse must come, too, because I feel him rock desperately, babble a few swear words, and then clutch me even closer as he pulsates deep inside me.

Afterward, we're a mess. The space between us is sticky and wet with come, sweat, and something that could be my tears, but I don't ever want to clean up. The last thing I can hear before falling asleep atop Jesse, his fingers fisted in my hair, is the slowing tempo of his heart.

■ ■ ■ ■ ■

"ARE YOU HUNGRY?" HE ASKS A COUPLE OF HOURS LATER AFTER the lodge has finally gone quiet.

I yawn into the curve of his throat. "No. Not really."

"Tell me if you are." He nuzzles the crown of my hair with his nose, and I decide that *he's* the most comfortable mattress in the universe—a perfect mix of soft and hard.

"What are you thinking?" I ask.

"Thinking?"

"Yeah, you know . . . Pondering. Ruminating. Contemplating. Musing. *Cogitating*." I kiss a spot at the base of his neck. "What are you *thinking*?"

"Nothing."

I snort softly. "You can't say nothing."

"Why not?"

"It's a felony."

"It's true, though." His smile widens against my temple. "I usually think about work, or what needs to be done, or whether I forgot to book my dental cleaning. Tonight, with you, I . . . this. *Now*." His fingers are still drawing patterns on my lower back. We've been so close, for so long, I should be all touched out, but with Jesse it's never too much. "What are *you* thinking?"

I grin into his skin. "About whether Otto and Mike are doing the same thing we're doing, right now."

"Christ." I can imagine Jesse's horrified expression. "Thank you for the mental image, Viola."

I giggle and fall asleep again, with a smile on my face.

■ ■ ■ ■ ■

I WAKE UP THE FOLLOWING MORNING, WHEN IT'S NO LONGER dark. Jesse's behind me under the covers, one of his hands curled around my breast. It's a pleasant weight that has even my bone marrow feeling warm and happy.

"Good morning," I tell him, wondering if he can hear the delight in my voice.

"Morning." His breath tickles the hair on my neck. A moment of hesitation, then his fingers tighten on me. "You smell unbelievably good."

It's because I smell like you, I think, though I doze off before the words make it out of my mouth.

When I wake again, Jesse's hand is pressing against my abdomen, and I've never been more turned on in my life. When I exhale a needy sigh, he easily eases inside me. He gets about halfway in, doesn't continue, and arousal wells up with every inch, an unstoppable tidal wave that makes my skin heat and tingle.

I hear an odd, foreign sound, and realize that it's my own moan.

"Okay?" Jesse asks, a gentle kiss over my shoulder. When I rasp out a "Yes," he shifts me until I'm lying half on my belly, his chest flush to my back. "Still okay?" he repeats, breath hot against my ear.

I bury my face in the pillow, confused by the pleasure. "It feels—" He pushes just half an inch deeper, hitting something soft and tender inside me. The feeling is devastating. Nuclear. "Sometimes I'm afraid that this might be too much for me."

"But it's not."

I nod, breathless. "But it's not."

He kisses the pulse at the base of my throat, and then lets his teeth graze against the vein there, as if to find the essence of me. "Hold tight. I'm gonna fuck you properly this time."

Last night seemed very proper to me, but I think I know what he means. He's in charge now. Taking his time, savoring every stroke, unhurriedly moving in and out. I'm tempted to push back against his cock, but instead close my eyes, stay still, and let the pleasure drift through me, breathing in Jesse's spectacular scent, thinking of dark green pine trees and fallen snow. "Did you use to think of us?" I ask him. "Of doing this? With me?"

His breath is loud, but even. He slides an arm under my head and pulls me closer. "All the time."

"What did you—*oh*—what did you imagine?"

"I don't know." His fingers slide lower, draw slow circles around my clit. "That you'd be soft, and warm, and wet. Beautiful. Funny. *Good*." He nudges a little deeper, and our breaths catch. "I expected a lot. But not . . . never this."

A perfect thrust, and pleasure tears through me. Jesse

keeps moving through my messy, mind-addling orgasm, and when I'm done he gives in and grabs his own. All throughout I hold his forearm, pressing soft, light kisses to the back of his hand.

■ ■ ■ ■ ■

"WHEN DID YOU FIRST READ THE LIMERENCE SERIES?" I ASK HIM after tucking my cheek against his chest. His palm sweeps lazily up and down my spine, over the small of my back, around my ass. I'm sure that he has counted my ribs twice already, and he let out a teasing smile when I confessed to being ticklish—as if storing up the anatomy of my body to reproduce a near-perfect replica inside his brain.

"About three years ago."

"That recently?"

"Yup." He turns his face just enough to press his nose into my hair and inhale deeply. In response, I rub my cheek into his skin.

"What made you pick it up?"

"A friend recommended it. Said I might like it. And it might help me."

"Help you?"

"Process my . . . feelings."

"Oh." I lift my head, propping my chin on my palm. My chest feels heavy when I try to imagine what was going on in Jesse's head for the past few years. I know he didn't just sit around and pine for me—he had girlfriends and friends and colleagues who love him, hobbies and interests and professional victories—but I cannot help regretting the misunderstanding of it all. "Did you tell them about . . . ?"

"Not the specifics. Just that there was someone I'd been liking for a while. That I wasn't in the position to make a move, and all I could do was . . . wait it out until it would fade." He smiles faintly. "She'd read the books when she was in her early teens and loved them. She recommended them to me, and I read them all in less than a week. And once I got to the end, I immediately restarted them."

I nod. "They're so different, once you know. Once you understand what the author was trying to do."

An ode to the enduring power of love. That's what Jesse said the other day, isn't it?

He lifts his hand and runs it through the length of my hair. I'm reminded of the care he took while undoing my braid last night. And of the pull on my scalp a few moments ago. "What about you? When did you discover the books?"

"My dad used to read them to me. When I was probably a bit too young for them, but I adored them anyway. Even the scarier, darker parts. I kind of forgot about them for a decade and a half. Then, when I was in college and he got sick, *I* read them back to him. And now . . . Well, he's gone. But Limerence was *our* thing, and since I inherited from him both my love for the series and my love for video games, and I think he'd be proud to know that his daughter might be the one who . . ." I swallow against the sudden obstruction in my throat. It takes me a moment to gather myself, but Jesse's warm hand stays, anchoring me. "That's why I need to get it right. It has to be absolutely perfect, but . . ."

"But?"

"I don't know. I've been going through my ideas . . ." I shake my head.

"I've seen your ideas, Viola. They look fantastic."

"I know they do," I say without conceit, and then briefly hesitate. Forty-eight hours ago, I would have gouged my eyes out before confessing any doubts to Jesse. But today he feels like my closest ally. I simply cannot imagine hiding anything related to Limerence from him. "Aqualuna was both Dad's and my favorite character. And I want to do her justice. But the stuff I've written so far hasn't quite captured her essence. I'm missing something, and I can't figure out what it is." I shrug. And then laugh, fully aware of how ridiculous I sound. "I'm overthinking it, right? I'm too attached to her."

Jesse cocks his head on the pillow. "I don't think you are. I feel protective of her, too. And of Noham."

I smile. "So nice of you, to pretend that I'm not a total weirdo."

"Anytime."

I pinch him lightly in retaliation, but the conversation is reminding me of something I would have considered earlier, if I hadn't been busy stuffing approximately a year's worth of sex into two days: Jesse's proposal to have Noham as a playable character.

Or, more exactly, my own reaction to it.

I can't believe that it had never occurred to me. Not that I would ever dare cut Noham out completely—Mike and Otto are *unbelievable*—but I'm starting to wonder if in my obsessive search for the real Aqualuna, I . . . "You know, I think I may have been neglecting him," I tell Jesse, suddenly serious.

He understands immediately what I'm referring to. "Noham?"

I nod as I work through my reasons. "The thing is, Noham and Aqualuna's love felt so . . . so beautiful, and powerful, but also doomed. Which, it is. *Literally* cursed. And the ending of the saga, it hurts. Knowing that everything Noham and Aqualuna go through together culminates in grief, it *hurts*." I'm talking to myself as much as to Jesse. Combing through mats of ideas and possibilities. "And since I love Aqualuna so much, since I want her to be happy for more than a handful of minutes, since it's a foregone conclusion that Noham's loss will break her heart, I've been . . . sidelining him. As if by reducing his role in her life, I could reduce her suffering. But her openness to loving him is such an important part of her character. If I take *that* away . . . Yes. That's it. That's why she fell flat. That's what's missing."

Jesse looks at me like he gets it. And it makes me want

to kiss him even more. "You know, maybe what we should do is—"

The knock at the door startles us. We exchange a long, silent glance. Then Jesse gets out of bed to pull on his plaid pajama pants and answer the door, while I duck under the covers and make myself as small as possible.

"Hey." From under the comforter, I can hear Mike's muffled voice. "You sick or something?"

"No."

"Oh. You look like you just got out of bed."

"I did. Slept in."

"Cool. You're still good with driving your car back, right?"

"Of course."

"Great. So, the streets look fine, at least as long as we go slowly. We're planning to leave at five."

A pause. "Okay."

"Thanks, dude. And oh, have you seen Viola?"

Jesse doesn't miss a beat. "Is she not in her room?" I'm starting to notice that he has mastered the art of sidestepping and non-answering questions.

"Nope. Maybe she went for a walk or something. I'll text her. See you later."

I wait for the sound of the closing door. A few seconds later, the mattress next to me dips. I emerge from the tangle of sheets and comforter, sitting upright while Jesse eyes me silently.

"I really enjoyed your performance as 'shapeless lump,'" he says, pushing my hair back from my face.

"Thank you. I hope to take it to Broadway soon." I force myself to smile, even if my cheeks object. "So I guess we *are* going home today, after all."

Jesse nods. He looks . . . yeah.

Exactly how I feel.

It's ridiculous that the prospect of returning to my quiet, empty apartment weighs in my belly like an iron boulder. And it's not that I think that this thing between us will be over once we go home, or that Jesse will ghost me as soon as we're back in Seattle. I know him better than that. But for the past two days it's been just us, suspended, locked away from reality, and now . . .

Well. Change is part of life, and all that shit.

"Guess this means I have to go pack," I say, fidgeting with a corner of the sheet.

Jesse nods, again.

"And you have to pack, too." I push the covers back. "I'll get out of your hair, so you can—"

His hand on my wrist pulls me back to him. He kisses what's left of that sentence out of my mouth—and kisses me, and kisses me, and *kisses* me, not stopping until I force myself to twist out of his embrace, even if it makes my heart heavy and my eyes prickly.

Chapter 17

THE RIDE BACK TO SEATTLE FEELS LIKE AN UPSIDE-DOWN version of the trip to the lodge.

I glance in Otto's direction, and notice that he *does* check Grindr, but only halfheartedly, and only once. For the most part, he reads the news, or plays *Flappy Bird* (with the sound off), or types something on his Notes app—just one word here, two words there. A love poem about Mike's elbow, perhaps. He even initiates several conversations with me, about several topics, and he doesn't seem miserable during any of them.

In the seat in front of mine, Ashley conks out half an hour into the car ride, snoring lightly and muttering something about koalas and chlamydia in her sleep that I cannot stop giggling at.

Jesse drives, quiet and pensive and handsome.

I traced that jaw at least a dozen times, I think, staring at his profile.

That little red burn at the base of his throat? I left it there.

It's a mark. It means that he's mine.

I lean back in my seat and look at his hands dwarfing the steering wheel, feeling content and warm. When my song comes on the radio, he turns up the volume a little.

I smile and close my eyes.

■ ■ ■ ■ ■

IT'S DARK WHEN WE PULL INTO THE COMPANY PARKING LOT. MY phone is long dead, but the clock on the dashboard says 9:37 p.m., and I have good reason to suspect that, unlike me, Jesse is a responsible person who actually set it back when Daylight Saving Time ended.

We are the last group to arrive—no doubt because I asked to stop for a restroom break. Ashley slept through it, Otto muttered something about pharmaceutical treatments for urinary incontinence that had no teeth whatsoever, and Jesse just pulled into the gas station's parking lot, going inside the store with me to buy a cup of black coffee for himself and a bag of Swedish Fish for me. I tuck what's left of it into the pocket of my coat and step into the freezing cold.

My car is where I left it four days ago, still a little beat up and a lot dirty. The sky is clear, but there are a few centimeters of white ice stuck to the roof and the windows—a sign that it must have snowed in the city, too. I open my trunk for Jesse to load the bag, and wipe the windshield as best I can. I lean against the driver's door, wondering if Ethan will need a ride, since we live in the same apartment complex.

Then I spot Mike coming my way.

"StarPlay called while I was driving back," he starts without preamble. "They wanted to know if we think we can work with Nephilim."

My heart takes a break from beating. "And you said . . ."

"That the retreat was a great success, and we are convinced that not only will a collaboration be possible, but also very fruitful." He pats my shoulder while I'm still trying to parse his words. "You and Jesse are going to be lead designers for *Limerence 3*. Congrats, Viola. I know how much this means to you, so I wanted you to be the first to know. I'll tell the rest of the team next week."

I watch him walk away, the shape of him blurred by the tears gathered in my eyes. *Dad,* I think. *I'm going to do such a great job.*

Around me, Nephilim and FlyButter employees are saying their goodbyes. Ethan chats with Shannon. Ashley laughs with Kai. A few feet from her, Jesse seems busy—first discussing something work-related with Otto and

Manny, then talking with Mike about something that makes them both smile, and after that helping Clara figure out why her car won't start. I try not to stare too much and limit myself to furtive glances. I don't want to leave without saying goodbye to him. I don't want to leave without *him*.

He'd hate that, too, if I disappeared. And the kicker is, among all the things we've done, it did not occur to us to exchange phone numbers. I don't even have his email. I guess I could get it from Mike, or my cousin's fiancé, but—

"Viola!" Ethan jogs up to me and lowers his voice. "I'm actually gonna go to, um, a friend's place tonight. Which means that I don't need a ride."

I smile. In a stage whisper, I reply, "Okay."

"I'll see you at work, 'kay?"

"Sure. Have fun with *not* Shannon."

He gives me the thumbs-up and walks away. I look at him and shake my head, making a mental note to remember this cloak-and-dagger ridiculousness for when I'm asked to give a toast at their wedding.

"Is your car all right?"

I whirl around. Jesse is standing right behind me, his breath a white puff in the cold air. Once again, no jacket.

"Do you need a ride?"

"Oh, no. I was waiting for Ethan since he lives so close to me. But it turns out that he's going to Shannon's and he doesn't need a ride." I shrug, then grin. "Want to beat him up a little for cheating on me?"

He stares at me flatly, and I giggle.

"Okay, then." Jesse presses his lips together, looking around the parking lot. Most people have left already, and the few remaining are getting in their cars. Mila drives past, waving at us with a tired smile. Otto is next, and if he thinks we don't see Mike in the passenger seat, he's deluded. I follow his Tesla with my gaze, shaking my head at his 8OTTO8 vanity plate.

"Did you know that I don't have your phone number?" I ask Jesse. "And that my phone is dead, so I can't even save it right now?"

"Shit. Lemme write it down for you." Jesse points vaguely in the direction of his car and spins on his heels, jogging away. He returns a few moments later, holding out a piece of paper that I readily accept.

I say, "By the way, full disclosure, to make sure we're on the same page . . . what I said at the lodge about loving your game, it was all true. *Zephyr's Blade* is definitely in my top three. And . . . I cannot wait to work on *Limerence* with you."

His lips twitch. "I meant it, too."

I cock my head. "You meant what?"

"What *I* said. At the lodge."

He said so many things. And yet, to ask him which one he is referring to would be nothing but dishonest of me. "Did you?"

He nods, his expression open and disarmed in a way that by now is as familiar to me as the scent of his skin. "About Aqualuna and Noham. And what you said earlier today."

I nod for him to go ahead, curious.

"I get it. Not wanting to set up the characters for inevitable heartbreak. How painful the ending of the saga is. So I was thinking that . . ."

"That when we build the game, we should write in a storyline, just one, in which the characters manage to break the curse and end up together?"

His eyes widen. "I . . . That's exactly what I was going to say. How did you know?"

I grin as I glance around at the now empty parking lot and the streets nearby. It's late, there is almost no traffic, and I have to count in my head to make sure that I have the day right.

Friday night. Which means that we have the weekend ahead of us. But even Monday—it doesn't sound bad. Not at all. Not now that I know whom I'll be working with.

I look at the crumpled piece of paper in my hand, open it, and frown. "This is not your number?"

"It's my address," he says. Not even a little sheepish.

"You don't need my number, Viola. Not for a while. Not if you let me keep you as close as I want to."

I hang my head low, laugh silently, and think, *Jesse fucking Andrews. I'm going to fall for you in the blink of an eye, and when I touch the ground, you better be right there with me.*

So I step into him. Lean my forehead against his chest. And when his arms close around me, I just say, "Let's take your car."

See Jesse meet Viola for the first time in this special bonus chapter!

Bonus Chapter

SHE'S THE ONE.

She's *the one*, and I know it from the start.

She may not have much experience—who does, at twenty-nothing?—and yet from the very first click I can see the raw talent. Her portfolio is unpolished but creative, engaging like no other candidate's. Nothing too flashy, but I lose myself in the walk-through of a narrative-driven puzzle game with a mechanic so unique, I can't figure out the building blocks of it. There are some samples of level design that I wish the people I currently work with were able to produce, a couple of original characters and their surprisingly authentic dialogue, infinite pools of ideas.

She's the one we have to hire, and for the better part of

an hour, I'm stuck in the timeless loop of the wonderful, different, fresh mind that created all of this. It's the chime of a notification that pulls me out of the flow, and I realize with a tinge of embarrassment that my nose is less than an inch from the monitor.

As always, very cool, Andrews.

I straighten and open the company Slack, finding a text from my boss.

KEVIN: **Did you get a chance to look at this batch of applicants for the Junior Dev position?**

JESSE: **Just now.**

KEVIN: **We should bring in #2, #17, and #35. Agree?**

I glance down at the list. None of the candidates Kevin mentioned has warranted a second look from me, but that's unsurprising, since I value inventiveness and originality, and he's into . . . I don't know, and at this point it's too late to ask.

Still, I'm happy to comply. I'm not going to fight him on this—not when I have my own ask to put forward.

JESSE: **Sure. And #12.**

KEVIN: **12 . . . Remind me, what was his name?**

I realize that I have no idea. I have to click out of the demo and navigate to the About Me section of the portfolio, which unfortunately is sparser than I'd like. Viola Bowen. Seattle native. Great education background, great internships. An interesting line about book-to-game adaptations that makes me want to pick her brain. There is a headshot of her that was obviously taken by someone with an iPhone—a brown-haired woman crossing her arms in front of a nondescript background. She seems young, probably because she is. Not quite smiling. Pretty in a way that, I have no doubt, hasn't done her many favors in this industry.

Her, I message Kevin, trying to swallow the irritation that always rises up my throat when he reminds me how much of a dickhead he is.

KEVIN: **?**

JESSE: **Not his name. Hers. And it's Viola Bowen.**

KEVIN: **Ah.**

KEVIN: **I don't know about that.**

JESSE: **?**

KEVIN: **We don't really have other female employees on the creative side. Is it a good idea to bring her in? She'd probably feel all alone and ganged up on, or something. Seems like courting trouble.**

I rub my face, in the throes of the intensely pleasurable daydream of screenshotting this conversation and using it to wallpaper the HR rep office. Then I remember that we don't fucking have an HR department. In no universe should I even be the one screening applications—I would like to spend my time designing games, not wrangling new hires. But we are a small studio. More important, we are an extremely poorly managed studio. Because we are managed by

Kevin, who, just like many other men in this industry, is an incompetent asshole who spent the last decade failing upward.

JESSE: Kevin, please reread what you wrote and tell me you see why it's problematic.

KEVIN: I guess.

I can almost hear his sigh. I'm sure it's not as deep as mine.

KEVIN: Sure. We can bring the girl in if you want.

I do want. In fact, I am excited about it. We set the interview for the following week and I spend large chunks of it on edge, half excited to finally meet her, half afraid that she'll be scooped up by a less shitty company in the interim. What if she starts looking outside of Seattle? Even if she stays, I know for a fact that FlyButter is hiring, or about to. Have they posted the ad yet? Mike is significantly more reasonable than Kevin. She'd be better off.

Still, when I email with her she seems delighted at the prospect of an in-person interview. I click through her portfolio more times than is necessary to get a good idea of a junior dev skill set, but I can't help myself. There is a tiny quirk in one of her characters' design that I'd love to ask about. What games did she grow up playing? What made her want to create her own? I *need* to know more about those book adaptations she mentioned.

We're mostly doing combat stuff here, and I like combat

stuff—fine, I love combat stuff—but even I have to admit it: Our last few works have been rote and boring. A new, brilliant brain could be exactly what the studio needs. If someone like her—Viola; Viola Bowen—were to come on board, maybe I wouldn't have to talk myself out of quitting once a week.

Yes. This could work.

Bottom line, my expectations for her are high. And still, when the morning of the interview comes, she blows them out of the water—in every possible way. Some of them, maybe not too good.

She comes in right on time, lingering in the entrance of the conference room. I'm busy cleaning my glasses on the hem of my shirt, which means that at the beginning I cannot make out much more than a shapely, dark-haired blob. Then I slide them up my nose, and my cool *collapses*.

She's not pretty. Or maybe she is, but she's also *more*. The most beautiful girl I've ever had the privilege to lay my eyes upon. She is . . . resplendent. Irresistible. Unique. The princess for whom the chosen warrior moves through the levels defeating guards, breaking out of dungeons, indefatigably conquering death. No, better than that: the princess who'll stick by the warrior's side and slay winged, sharp-toothed beasts to help him clear the path out of the fortress. Yes. Much more to my taste.

If someone asked me to explain why, I wouldn't be able

to say *what* is so striking about her. But it doesn't make her pull on me any less strong. I can only stare and experience the feeling that's right *there*, in the air surrounding her—a gestalt impression of perfection that should be too dangerous to truly exist.

It's nine in the morning, and I may be fucked for life.

She walks toward us, and I jerk awake. Reflexively, not really knowing what I'm doing, I stand to shake her small, cool hand. The entire process takes no longer than a couple of seconds, but it's enough for me to write a whole movie treatment about what the rest of our lives together could look like, complete with training montage. I see dates in ramen restaurants next to comic stores, epic tabletop campaigns, heart emojis discreetly dropped in Discord DMs; I see heated arguments over who we should be romancing in *Baldur's Gate 3*, sleepy nights spent pressed to each other watching different streamers together, a first anniversary celebrated by buying her a ridiculously expensive headset.

I have no time to imagine further, and thank fuck. I sit back down next to Kevin, sure that I must be having one of those transient strokes that are not a big deal but mess up your brain anyway. I'm usually much more grounded than this. I pace myself. I don't play house in my head with future colleagues.

Even though she's not going to be. A few minutes into the interview, and I know it. Once I'm no longer too stupefied by the tiny mole on her cheek and the rasp of her contralto to pay attention, it becomes obvious that Viola Bowen is *not* going to be working with me anytime soon.

Because Kevin, as usual, is fucking shit up.

I hear him heavily imply that our studio might be too *manly* for her, and my brain buzzes with alarm. Then I hear him say it outright, and the rest happens very quickly: Viola's contemptuous look, my sharp reminder to Kevin that being a piece of shit should not be his default mode.

All I want is to save this interview. I'm ready to go on my knees and apologize on behalf of this dickhead. To offer his testicles on a PS5 platter as a sign of goodwill. To swear to her that if she accepts the position I will personally make sure that she'll never have to interact with him—in fact, what if I stick around her the whole time, just to make the transition easier? I could be her personal bodyguard. Shield her from this bullshit. It sounds like a great job description.

But it's too late. Viola is already out the door.

"You are worthless, Kevin," I say. I follow her out before I can hear his reaction, jogging through the lobby to catch up.

Slower, I tell myself. *Slow down*. Nobody likes being harassed *and* chased in the span of thirty seconds. But I'm so panicked that she'll disappear into Seattle's foggy air, I simply can't stop myself, not until I'm standing in front of her. With the left part of my brain, I'm drafting my resignation letter, mentioning Kevin's incompetence every other line. With the right . . .

Which part of the brain falls in love at first sight?

"Hey—hey." I block her path with my body. When her eyes lift up to meet mine, electricity runs through me. "Are you okay?"

She snorts. "Should I be?"

"No. You absolutely shouldn't."

"Good. Because your boss is a shithead."

"Oh, I know."

I study her serious mouth. The frown between her eyebrows. There are dark circles under her eyes that tell me she hasn't slept much. Her clothes are wrinkled, and she's pressing a palm to her temple as if to shoo away a headache. She seems to be going through it.

Still, I take a step back. Because here's a fact: Even though Viola Bowen is younger and less experienced and obviously bedraggled, I feel a little intimidated by her.

We're in dream-girl territory here.

"Kevin is appalling, and you have every right to say it."

"Yeah, well. Unfortunately, he also holds the key to the job of my dreams, so."

The defeat in her voice depresses me. To the point that what comes out of my mouth is full-on self-sabotage. "No, he doesn't."

"Excuse me?"

"You're better than this job, Viola."

Her eyebrow arches. "How so?"

"I've seen your portfolio." I swallow. "There are other studios. And they'd suit you much better."

For the first time since stepping into the interview, she looks at me with a glimmer of interest. All at once, I am a part of her world, a part whose existence is being acknowledged and assessed. I want to be found worthy so badly, my heart beats faster.

"Are they hiring, though?" Viola cocks her head, and I may be having a religious experience. "Those other studios?"

"They will be. Soon."

"Who?"

Her attention on me is addling. Drug-like. Probably the reason I don't feel any pain as I proceed to shoot myself in the foot by telling Viola about FlyButter, then by giving her a few pointers to beef up her portfolio and appeal to Mike. I try to keep my distance, not to stare too much. She seems exhausted. She *is* exhausted, going by the way her face stretches into a wide yawn. She doesn't need me crowding her.

"Sorry! I'm so tired today—can't believe I stayed up so late to prep to impress that asshole."

"Don't worry about that," I say. And the rest tumbles out like a natural catastrophe, at the worst time and place. There is nothing I can do to stop it when I hear myself ask, "Would you like to get coffee?"

I wouldn't say that I usually have a lot of game, but I've successfully asked out enough girls that I know to be mortified by how my words sound. It's the way the question comes out, too fast and entirely out of place. Egregiously inappropriate. Embarrassing. It's just—her voice, the way she talks with her hands, the collar of her shirt that falls just a little askew . . . She might be the most inviting thing I've ever experienced, and I can see it, her, us, talking for hours about her next steps, about the Kevins of the world, about what makes a successful D&D campaign, about absolutely nothing—

"Oh, no. No, don't worry. Not going to fall asleep at the wheel. 'Cause I can't afford a car, yet."

She smiles for the first time and I'm blinded. Almost bowled over. The high that comes from it is some very, *very* good shit—until the meaning of her words registers.

"Ah."

The refusal hits me almost physically, but I manage not to slither backward and to keep my expression composed. Of course, *no*. What the fuck was I thinking, asking her out after the shitshow that just went down?

But I wasn't. Thinking. I was too busy *wanting*. "I'm sorry. I have to apologize—"

"Nah, unless you're a ventriloquist and Kevin is secretly a puppet, it's not your fault."

I'm sure that she doesn't understand what I'm apologizing for. But then she continues on, telling me the shit that happened this morning is not even the worst she's been through from men in our industry, and the longer she talks, the more it feels like a warning to get away from her—one that *I* obviously deserve.

And still, an *If you change your mind* is on the tip of my tongue.

I'm not even certain what I'm offering. *If you change your mind, that coffee is still on the table. If you change your mind, you only have to say. If you change your mind, I'll probably drop everything. Snap your fingers—just like that.*

But none of it is what I should tell her. So I settle, just a few minutes later, for echoing her *"See you around."* I watch Viola walk out of the lobby, hair bouncing with new confidence and hope, hand waving at me through the glass door as she hurries to cross the street while the light is still green. Swallow my disappointment and take a deep breath.

Okay. So maybe Viola Bowen is *not* the one.

Even if, for a while, it really felt like she could be.

Acknowledgments

So grateful to my Spotify team (Henna Silvennoinen, Bethany Strout, Colleen Prendergast, Rinn Kraus, Leah Kleynhans, Jeffrey Jordan, Christopher Sutton, Taylor Barnes, Jessica Dugan, Kate Dilyard, and Chantelle Young) and my Berkley team (Sarah Blumenstock, Liz Sellers, Cindy Hwang, Vikki Chu, Daniel Brount, Jennifer Myers, Christine Legon, Bridget O'Toole, Kim-Salina I, Kristin Cipolla, Tawanna Sullivan, and Christine Ball), as well as Kelsey Navarro Foster for narrating the audiobook. As usual, a thousand thanks to lilithsaur for the most beautiful cover, and to Thao for the most beautiful agenting. Special thanks to Shep for the gaming consulting, to S. for additional gaming consulting, and to Jessica Story-Johnson and her hubby for that super helpful brainstorming sesh in Belmont.

Justin Murphy of Out of the Attic Photography

ALI HAZELWOOD is the #1 *New York Times* bestselling author of *Problematic Summer Romance* and *The Love Hypothesis*, as well as a writer of peer-reviewed articles about brain science, in which no one makes out and the ever after is not always happy. Originally from Italy, she lived in Germany and Japan before moving to the US to pursue a PhD in neuroscience. When Ali is not at work, she can be found crocheting, eating cake pops, or watching sci-fi movies with her three feline overlords (and her slightly-less-feline husband).

VISIT ALI HAZELWOOD ONLINE

AliHazelwood.com

AliHazelwood

AliHazelwood